TARGETING TELEPATHY

THE TELEPATH TRILOGY BOOK THREE

STEFON MEARS

Thousand Faces Publishing

Also by Stefon Mears

Cavan Oltblood Series
Half a Wizard
The Ice Dagger
Spells of Undeath

Spells for Hire
Devil's Shoestring
Zombie Powder
Spirit Trap
Dragon's Blood (coming December 2019)

The Rise of Magic
Magician's Choice
Sleight of Mind
Lunar Alchemy
Three Fae Monte
The Sphinx Principle

The Telepath Trilogy
Surviving Telepathy
Immoral Telepathy
Targeting Telepathy

Edge of Humanity
Caught Between Monsters
Hunting Monsters

Power City Tales
Not Quite Bulletproof
No Money in Heroism

Devil's Night
Portal-Land, Oregon
Stealing from Pirates
Fade to Gold
With a Broken Sword
Twice Against the Dragon
The House on Cedar Street
Sudden Death
On the Edge of Faerie
Confronting Legends (Spells & Swords Vol. 1)
Uncle Stone Teeth and Other Macabre Poems
The Patreon Collection, Vol. 1-4 (Vol. 5, coming soon)

Published by Thousand Faces Publishing, Portland, Oregon

http://1kfaces.com

ISBN: 978-1-948490-03-0

TARGETING TELEPATHY

THE TELEPATH TRILOGY - BOOK THREE

BERKELEY TELEPATHIC OUTREACH GUIDELINES

1. If you pick up a thought without trying, you might as well have overheard it being spoken.
2. Read minds with caution. You're better off not knowing most people's secrets.
3. Control minds with caution. Try not to break anyone.
4. If you do break someone's mind, fix them. You may need help to do so.
5. Don't rely on telepathy for everything.
6. Zero tolerance for megalomaniacs.

1

"YOU'RE CHEATING, AREN'T YOU?"

Some people will complain about anything.

I'm sitting in a field-level seat at AT&T park, right behind home plate. It's a beautiful June Saturday afternoon. Wisps of glowing white clouds in the pale sky above. The crowd is clapping and chanting, "Beat L.A.!" with that stadium echo like distant thunder. Gentle breezes are coming in from McCovey Cove, carrying the ubiquitous scent of hot dogs and peanuts to contrast the taste of my own garlic fries.

The seats are incredible. I don't want to think of how much these season tickets must cost. They're a business perk for my parents, who frequently have to entertain the politically important. Often, when my parents don't need them, they get passed on to staffers and others as rewards for jobs well done.

And once in a while, like today, I get to claim them and bring my best friend to watch the Giants beating the Dodgers six-to-one in the third.

Correction: the Giants are beating the Dodgers' ace, Clay Kersey, *the Cy Young Award winning southpaw*, six-to-one in the third. What's more, the Giants have runners on first and third with two out, and the heart of the order coming up. The game is paused though, while the Dodger pitching coach is out at the mound trying to figure out what's wrong with his star pitcher.

Meanwhile, in the seat next to me, my best friend Tony Gottschalk has figured out what that poor, beleaguered coach could never begin to guess, and finally gotten around to asking the question I've been expecting since the first inning.

I turn to Tony. He doesn't have a jersey like I do, but he's got his ever-expanding mop of black curls tucked under his Giants cap, and his unlicensed orange and black tee-shirt reads "My team isn't the only thing that's Giant."

"How could I be cheating?" Mock innocence all through my voice. "I'm not even playing."

"Rick..."

I wiggle my eyebrows and draw a long pull from my insanely huge cup of Limon Blast soda.

"Dude!"

"Hey," I say, setting the cup down on the cement, "is it my fault he's having trouble concentrating today? Maybe he can't take his eyes off the knockout blonde ten seats down."

"He pitches in L.A. He's used to seeing *movie stars* behind the plate."

"And yet, I can't help feeling as though his mind isn't quite on the game."

It helps that I've been feeding him psychic static. Not much, just little distractions at key points in his windup. It's really easy, with the excited buzz of forty-something thousand minds around me. Most of them Giants fans, but a sizable enough number of Dodgers fans to provide a good conflicting morass where the gestalt — the merging point of what I think of as individual fogs of thoughts — clashes.

Well, all right. I haven't quite stopped there. Every so often a Giants batter has also just happens to have a completely accurate hunch about what pitch is coming and to what part of the strike zone.

After all, what's the point of being a telepath if I never let myself have any fun at all?

"I hate the Dodgers as much as any Giants fan," says Tony, "but do you have so little faith in your team that you want them to win like this?"

"Every game? No. Most games? No. But did you read the things this guy said about the Giants in the paper this morning?"

"You still read the paper?" Tony shakes his head at a slight angle as though commiserating. "Still not in in the twenty-first century, huh? Well, don't worry. You'll get here."

"Hey. I like the feel of newsprint."

"You and newspaper publishers. The rest of us have moved on."

"Wait." I narrow my eyes at the subject change. "So you're cool with this?"

"You didn't exactly ask my permission, and I wouldn't do it if I were in your shoes, but of all the ways you could possibly abuse your power, this strikes me as one of the least offensive."

Considering we know of a telepath who re-arranged a married couple's life to suit his own needs for sex and living arrangements, and another who completely shattered a girl's mind by forcing her to fall in love with him, that's damning with faint praise.

Of course, neither of those two are telepaths anymore. I saw to that, personally. Went right into their heads and cut off access to their powers in the most permanent fashion I could muster.

I may not mind messing with a baseball game, but we're talking about people's lives here.

Tony and I put together the Blackhall-Gottschalk Code of Telepathic Conduct to help me avoid abusing people with my power. And with the minds of basically everyone in the world open and available to me, abuses could escalate quickly without some kind of measuring stick to evaluate what I'm doing.

"So you consider this abuse?"

"The reason you just gave violates rule 4.2," says Tony, his voice quieter now, though I can tell that no one sitting nearby is paying attention to us. "You're only doing this for entertainment, which we agreed is not enough reason to mess with a person's mind."

"True, though I am getting a training benefit out of it, which means 4.3 applies."

"How?" Tony's attention is intense, and I wonder if his Zen practice has begun giving him benefits beyond his superhuman driving skills.

I have to think about that for a moment before I can explain, so I stuff a couple of garlic fries in my mouth. They've been sitting there long enough to get soggy, but the garlic is still strong and oily on my tongue.

After I swallow, I lower my voice to just above a whisper.

"The normal way to do this is like when we were playing pool that time. Send images or phrases into his head. Like if I made him think about that blonde." I give my head a slight shake. "I'm trying something different though. I'm feeding him awareness of the conflicts between the amalgamated gestalts of the Giants and Dodgers fans."

Tony blinks fast, surprise all through his aspect. Meanwhile, the umpire has broken up the sermon on the mound, and the pitching coach has retreated to the dugout. In the background I can see two pitchers up and working fast in the Dodger bullpen.

"Holy shit." Tony has forgotten to be quiet, but his amazement only draws a little amusement. "You can do that?"

"Apparently. I haven't done it before. It was just an idea."

"Well, it's definitely practice then." I can feel Tony thinking about this. The implications. "Jesus, Rick. I don't think I quite appreciated your versatility."

It is impressive, says a mind I do not know, which means a telepath I don't know, making contact. *Do you have a moment to chat?*

THE GIANTS GAME IS UNDERWAY AGAIN, BUT I'M TOO DISTRACTED TO get back to messing with the Dodgers' starting pitcher. Tony can see the shock in my expression at the unexpected telepathic contact, but I wave off any concern with a quick hand-movement.

Tony, being Tony, immediately gets that it's a telepath thing, and goes back to his garlic fries and watching the game. He settles his skinny frame onto the hard plastic seat like it's a big, comfy armchair.

What do I know about this strange telepath? Mental voice sounded male, and that's tough to disguise. No particular emotional subtext to that first sending, which means good control. He also had to have been paying attention to my conversation with Tony without my noticing.

In other words, he's better than I am.

All right, Rick. Enough with the paranoia.

—*Hi. I'm Rick Blackhall. Good to meet you, and I hope you aren't a Dodgers fan.*—

I let my subtext convey a slight sense of amused embarrassment. Like a sheepish grin.

Pleased to meet you, Rick. My name is Hyun-Ki Noh. And honestly I consider sports fandom one step up from barbarism, so it doesn't matter to me if you interfere. I'm just here entertaining a client.

Blunt honesty underlies his words, but I appreciate that. Most of the telepaths I've met so far have wanted to play games.

I have a sense of where he is now. About three rows behind me, and one section down the first base line. I check myself from glancing.

I would have settled for focusing the pitcher's mind on that pretty blonde ten seats down from you.

—*She drew your attention from where you're sitting?*— I don't try to hide my disbelieving undercurrent.

No, but some of the men around you are paying as much attention to her as to the game.

True. I've noticed that myself.

And the pitchers can see her clearly over the umpire's right shoulder, so it would have been easy. An undertone of respect accompanies the rest of his thought. *I like your technique better though. Mind if I steal it?*

—*Help yourself. Just tell me how you tuned in. I didn't pick you up, so you couldn't have been watching my thoughts or Tony's.*—

I wasn't. I felt the ripples of your interactions with that pitcher and traced them to you. Then I tuned into the heavy-set gentleman sitting behind you, and listened to your conversation through his ears. Don't worry, though. I kept him from noticing you or what you and your friend were saying. I won't do anything to draw attention to you. In return, though I expect you'll want to mention this conversation to your friend Tony, I'd appreciate your keeping my identity out of it.

—Of course.— Time to work in the important part of this conversation. If I can see an easy way to do it. —*You seem pretty casual about finding another telepath.*—

I can't be the first other you've met.

Ahoy, Captain! Segue off the starboard bow!

—*Actually, I'm a member of the Berkeley Telepathic Outreach, and I'd love to tell you about our little group.*—

I still think it's a terrible name. But after more than a semester of meetings with Jamal, Mary and Terrence, it was the best we could agree on. We couldn't settle on much in the way of rules either. Mary's too pro-power and Terrence is too anti-telling-people-what-to-do. Hell, even Jamal wants looser restrictions on our members than I do.

But it's a start.

I send Hyun-Ki a memory of the introductory spiel and the guidelines, and give him time to sort through them. In the meantime, the Giants are back on the field and the Dodgers are batting. Two out and nobody on, but I'm a little disappointed that the Giants couldn't continue the rally without me.

Maybe Tony has a point about too much interference being unsportsmanlike.

I'm still not sorry.

"There's another telepath here," I say to Tony while the crowd around us cheers a called strike. "One I don't know."

"Hope he's not a Dodgers fan."

Tony can't help looking around, but I reassure him with a calming hand.

"He's not. And right now it doesn't matter where he is. I sent him the BTO stuff."

"And now, let me guess. He ain't seen nothing yet."

I sigh. "Will you let that go?"

"You're right. You guys are taking care of business. And I mean every day."

"You're being an asshole."

He laughs, completely unabashed. "Dude, you're the ones who came up with an acronym that's been associated with a classic rock band since the 70s."

"How do you even know that? Does your car only pick up stations from the year it was made?"

Tony starts to respond, but I lose the thread when Hyun-Ki makes contact again.

Interesting. Regular meetings, and the opportunity to practice some of the trickier aspects of our gift. I will take your offer under consideration. May I contact you again?

—Of course. Take all the time you need.—

He breaks contact, and I come back in the middle of Tony going on about the power and majesty of Storm Warning, his restored mid-80s Rambler. He's gotten loud enough that I can feel the irritation of the fans around us. Having their attention "forced" from the game and their other interests to the ranting of a nineteen-year-old bragging about his car.

"Dude!" I say, cutting him off mid-sentence. "I know you and that car are some sort of sublime combination, but someone's going to call an usher."

In fact, someone has. I can feel the determined approach of a sixty-something woman with a grandmotherly demeanor and a drill sergeant heart. She only has a warning in mind, but she intends to keep an eye on us after she issues it.

Which is something I don't need — scrutiny in a public place.

Can't afford anything as overt as telling her we aren't the droids she's looking for. Someone around us would notice...

I'm just considering how to ease her focus off of us and onto someone else when I feel another telepathic contact. This one's formal. Polite. Like someone knocking on my mind, to see if I have a moment to talk.

I recognize the knock. Jamal. Recent Psychology graduate from Berkeley (where I'll be a sophomore this fall), and member of the Berkeley Telepathic Outreach. I open my focus.

His thoughts come fast and upset. Steam room moist heat.

I need you to come to me. Mary's dead.

2

———

You know how, when your alarm wakes you up, every once in a while you can hit the snooze button and in the five minutes between buzzes you can fall back asleep and dream a whole two-hour movie's worth of epic adventure? Deep telepathic conversation is that fast. Or faster.

Doesn't have to be telepaths on both ends, either. If I go deep enough into someone's head, anything I do happens that fast. I once felt as though I took nearly a week to try to fix the psychic damage to this girl's mind, and it turned out to only be a couple of minutes. And even that was because I had to keep coming back up to her surface thoughts.

The point is that deep telepathic conversation happens at what I call dream speed, and what other people call the speed of thought.

So I don't even need to explain myself to Tony before projecting my focus deep into Jamal's mind. No one would see me staring off into space or twitching and shaking like I'm having a fit or anything obnoxious like that. And unlike my surface conversation with Hyun-Ki Noh, when I get back I won't have missed so much as a pitch.

Not that the game matters at the moment.

Mary's dead.

I can't believe Jamal would lie about that, but I can't quite believe it either. It just seems, I don't know...

I never liked her much, to be honest. When we met she had no issues with warping people to serve her needs. Not as bad as Stephen the megalomaniac or Kelly, who broke a girl making her "love" him. But still.

She did get better over the course of the last semester. But she and I were never really going to be friends. Too much history at that point. I mean, she once had me threatened by these two campus cops she used to keep as errand boys and sex toys, despite one of them being married.

Anyway, usually Jamal likes to meet people in the image of a television diner from the Fifties, so everyone can enjoy the taste of chiliburgers and chocolate milkshakes without the consequences. But not today.

When I reach for his mind I find myself standing in a windy cemetery. The grave markers are worn and ragged, and grass grows uneven and wild everywhere. Twisted oak trees, naked of their leaves, seem to mark the rows. Everything smells like wood smoke and candied apples.

Jamal's personal image profile is half-sitting on a rounded raw stone grave marker. He's wearing a muted purple shirt over black pants, and a black duster over it. Usually his PIP's skin is that pure African blue-black, but today it's closer to his body's deep brown. His curls are close-shorn, just like they were the last time I saw him in person. His PIP is a little taller that his real body though, maybe six-four instead of six-two, and at a glance I'd say even more athletic.

People always tell me my own PIP just looks like me. Skinny, not too tall, short black hair. Maybe better looking that I really am, but I'm not the best judge of that. I know I'm still wearing my Giants hat and jersey, which almost makes me feel silly.

"Where is this place?"

"It's not real. I got the image from a novel I read back in high school. Gothic stuff." He points down past the edge of the cemetery to a little road. "If you take that south for about ten minutes you'd come to a castle. In the book anyway."

He looked up into the overcast sky. "Seemed appropriate."

"I didn't think you and Mary were that close," I say.

"She started getting more reasonable last semester. Acting like more of a person and less of a bitch queen. Even released Pete and Repeat and took the time to straighten out their heads."

"Seriously?" I didn't know about that last part.

"She needed my help, but whatever. I think maybe you and I were finally getting through to her." Jamal shakes his head. "Either way, she was one of us. Only four of us, and now we're three."

Sadness underlies his thoughts. I feel a little guilty that I don't feel sadder, because right now I don't feel much of anything. Maybe I'm just in shock. Hard to believe one of us could just die like that. I mean we're telepaths, not immortals, but still.

"How did it happen?"

"It was a mugging. Can you believe it?" Jamal lights up a clove cigarette, despite the fact that I've never seen him smoke before, either in person or in anyone's head. "I'll tell you the rest when Terrence gets here."

"Is Darcy coming?"

Jamal snorts out smoke at the question. Of course not. Not only did Darcy choose not to join our little forming community, she considered Mary beneath contempt, both as a person and as a telepath.

Darcy might be a better telepath than any of us or all of us. She has a subtlety to her approach that I can't begin to match. Mary was almost her opposite. Overt where Darcy is understated. Rough and untalented where Darcy is brilliant. Darcy won't miss Mary in the least.

Terrence appears two graves down from me. He's another one who looks just like his PIP. About my height and slightly rumpled in his faded shirt and jeans, but with his Chinese ancestry, no one is ever likely to confuse the two of us.

He also grew up in Los Angeles a lifelong Dodger fan, so my hat and jersey earn me a raised eyebrow as he nods his greeting. I can feel that he wants to ask if I'm at the game, wants to know if I'm the reason for the score, but knows this isn't the time for questions.

Terrence materializes a jeans jacket and dons it against the persistent wind.

"Nice timing," says Jamal. "I was just about to tell Rick what happened."

"Pete and Repeat figured out what she did to them and came looking for revenge?" says Terrence.

Pete and Repeat were what Mary called Pete LeMaster and Pete Jefferson, the two U.C. Berkeley campus cops she twisted to her liking.

"I don't think so," says Jamal, blowing out a plume of white smoke. "If so, they disguised it as a mugging. Reminds me, though. I want to check on them and see how their recovery is coming along."

"Let me know if you want a hand," I say, buttoning up my jersey against the wind, which seems to have gotten colder since I got here. "So what exactly did happen? How did she let herself get mugged?"

"Simple." Terrence shrugs. "She was never good enough to notice casual thoughts without effort. She probably never saw the mugger coming."

"I don't buy it. The instant the mugger said, 'Gimme your money,' she'd have been in his head like an icepick."

"Well," says Jamal, "you guys *could* listen to the one of us who's read the minds of the reporting police."

He flicks his cigarette in the air and it vanishes.

Terrence and I look at him.

"According to a witness, the mugger had a partner. Another guy with a pistol some ten feet behind him and in the shadows. She didn't get a good look."

"Mary?" I ask.

"The witness. Florence Caravella. Says she was down the block loading some clothes into her trunk when she saw the first guy pull a gun on Mary. Heard him demand money. Then he hesitated. Started raising the gun to his own temple."

"Typical Mary," mutters Terrence, "ready to kill a would-be mugger rather than look for the non-violent solution."

"May I finish?" Jamal folds his arms and waits until Terrence gives him an apologetic nod.

"So the mugger is putting the gun to his own head, then the witness hears a gunshot. But it's not the mugger blowing his brains out. It's a muzzle flash in the shadows behind a sedan parked ten feet farther down. Mary drops to the pavement. Dead."

"Dead on contact?" Terrence scratches at his shoulder. "Where was she hit?"

"Bullet came in through her right eye. Took most of the back of her head when it came out."

I'm shuddering at the thought when Terrence says, "Must have been a hollow point. Why would a mugger use a hollow point?"

"What happened to the first mugger?" I ask. I'm still shivering at the idea, and I have an urge to pat the back of my head for reassurance.

"Oh, he pulled the trigger. His wasn't a hollow point though. He's not even dead. Just unconscious in a hospital bed. Second mugger disappeared. Never even robbed her."

Neither Terrence nor I get more than a surprised grunt out before Jamal says, "Witness cried out at the gunshot. Thinks she scared off the second mugger. Cop whose head I was in thinks it's likely."

"Armed robbery may be a felony," says Terrence, "but you don't get life or the death penalty for it."

"A mugger." Jamal spits. "She was killed by a mugger. *A mugger!*"

"A mugger with a partner," I add. "How common is that?"

"It happens," says Terrence. "Tag teaming. Confusing witnesses and victims. Not common in Berkeley, but I've heard of a few teams doing it in Oakland and Richmond. Could be one of them branching out."

"Why have you heard of any?"

"I volunteer around the police station. Help the innocent avoid problems and help the guilty find their way into cells. Just little things here and there. A guilty guy slips up in his alibi. Confesses some element that points to a key fact he'd been trying to hide. Meanwhile, evidence chains get screwed up for the innocent, or a cop decides they aren't worth the paperwork."

"That's brilliant," says Jamal, and I nod along with him.

Terrence shakes off the compliment. "Can't aid as many as I'd like, but it helps me sleep at night."

"So what about Mary?" I breathe out a long sigh. "Her parents are probably going nuts. Should we go to the funeral?"

Jamal and Terrence are both shaking their heads before the no's start leaving their mouths.

"I am not answering the how-did-you-know-Mary question," says Jamal, "and you don't want to either."

He has a point.

"How about I find out when it will be and we hold our own little tribute?"

That, they'll agree to.

"Anything else before I get going?" says Terrence.

"I've met another telepath at the Giants game. Hyun-Ki Noh. Might be interested in joining."

"So you *are* at the Giants-Dodgers game..." starts Terrence, but Jamal cuts him off.

"My brother Jice isn't into the idea of joining a group. He says that if we manage to build something real over the next couple of years, maybe he'll join us then. Right now he says it feels too much like a kids club."

"Are you messing with the players?" says Terrence.

"Gotta get back," I say. "Hyun-Ki might have some questions."

I GET BACK INTO MY OWN HEAD, WHICH IS STILL SITTING IN A TERRIFIC seat at the Giants game. I haven't missed a pitch. Literally. The pitcher was in his windup when I left, and I'm back in time to see the final strike of the third out cross the plate.

That old lady usher is still coming to talk to us, but I just feed her the memory of doing so. She thinks she was firm, but fair, and that Tony and I both sounded chagrined when we apologized and promised to keep it down.

That might not satisfy the person who called her over, but if they raise a stink, I'll handle that too. I'm in no mood for that crap.

It's still a beautiful day and the Giants are still beating the Dodgers, but it's not as much fun anymore. Sadness has started welling in my gut. Mary may have been more like a bad co-worker than a friend, but still, I knew her. And now she's dead. Somebody shot her.

And Jamal was right. She was getting better. Relaxing her false front through the course of the semester. Smiling and laughing with us more instead of trying to compete at everything. She even released poor, abused Pete and Repeat, and she no longer pretended there were others out there under her secret control. Her "sleeper agents" she once called them. Back when she pretended to have them.

I can still remember her confessing the truth at one of our in-person meetings at Sufficient Grounds, a little coffee shop off of Telegraph in Berkeley. She was sitting there in a hot pink mini sundress, trying her best to look like Pacific Islander Barbie, sipping her double-mocha latté and saying, "I don't really run around planting suggestions deep in people's minds. That was just ... we used to be so competitive, you know?"

I couldn't let that go without asking about Amaris. She who had been my apex goth girlfriend for a good six months. Amaris had been fiercely in love with me right up until I confessed I was a telepath. Then it was all about paranoia and wondering how she could ever know her feelings were real.

Ironic, considering how we met.

"Oh. Well. Yes, Amaris was my test case," Mary admitted, even then without a trace of shame. Jamal might claim otherwise, but she never showed me any trace of shame or regret over anything she did. "I got her good and wound up for you. That was it though. The rest was all you." She drew an exaggerated X across her ample cleavage. "Cross my heart."

Then she fluttered her eyes and we were all laughing, but it was all right because Mary was laughing too.

She had her moments.

"Earth to Rick," says Tony. "You in there? Not like you to miss a Dodger strikeout without taunting the batter."

"Mary's dead." I catch him up on everything.

"What are you going to do?"

"Check on Pete and Repeat, along with Jamal." I shrug. "Other than that, nothing *to* do. I'm not exactly a cop. If I get involved I'll just get in the way. I'll leave the investigation to the professionals."

I settle in to watch the game, even if my heart is no longer in it. But Tony's right about one thing. I feel like I need to do something. There's got to be some way I can help. I just need to figure out what it is.

3

It's around six when Tony's old Rambler speed-slithers through the streets of Long Pine City like a supersonic rattlesnake heading for my house.

Every so often I have to remind myself that Long Pine City *is* a city. Heck, it's a county seat. But when I was growing up, there were still parts of downtown that were fields instead of parking lots or trendy boutiques. Not many, but still.

It felt too small to be a city. More like a town. The Cultural Commission always seemed more important than the City Council itself, much less the mayor. We had a twenty-minute-long freight train that came through town at five o'clock every weekday, because who cared? It wasn't like we had a rush hour. And the local paper?

Six pages long.

Six pages.

Think about that a second. San Jose has the Mercury News, with thick sections and ads and comics and everything. San Francisco has the Chronicle — or is it the Examiner? They used to have both, but I think one of them folded. Either way, again thick papers with lots of news. These papers cover national and international events, sports, all kinds of things.

The Long Pine City Tribune covers ... Long Pine City. Hey, look, there were some arrests on page four. Here's page six, where the local public high schools can pretend their sports teams matter.

See what I mean? Long Pine City may be a city in the strictest sense of the word, but it sure doesn't feel like a modern American city. Heck, our total population wouldn't fill some football stadiums.

And when I say the streets of Long Pine City, I'm talking about a place where the downtown isn't more than a mile square. I can go from my house in the foothills through downtown and out to 101, at the speed limit, in ten minutes if I hit the lights.

So, really, there's no reason at all for Tony to slip between cars and take orange lights at speeds that should make an old rust bucket like Storm Warning vibrate apart from sheer frustration.

Except that he's Tony, and this is how he drives.

Which is why the front passenger seat has an after-market oh-shit bar. I insisted. In fact, I'm clutching it right now.

As usual.

"Tony," — I'm surprised at how casual my voice sounds against the blaring of car horns — "I'm pretty sure that was a red light."

He smirks at me. "Was the intersection clear?"

"Yes, but—"

"Next question."

"But it was *right in front of a cop!*"

"Do you hear a siren?"

I think about that while Tony whips around an unnecessary corner to make the drive last a little longer. I swear the two tires on my side of the car catch air as he does.

"No. No I don't."

"Next que—"

"Tony!" I sputter before I can get my next words to come out with anything like coherence. "That was a cop and you've *got* to be felony speeding. *How?*"

"The road can't commit a felony."

"No. Seriously."

"Rick, all these years and you still don't get it," he says, and despite my own near-infarction level of stress, his whole aspect radiates peace and calm. "No accidents. No tickets. When I'm in the driver's seat, I *am* the road. It's my place of Samādhi."

Trees, blocks and parked cars fly past us on both sides, even on the narrow side streets as we get closer to my home. His odd patterns avoid stop signs entirely, and now that we're away from the lights and moving through neighborhoods, apparently other moving cars as well.

"Take your meditation more seriously," he continues, looking at me and not the street ahead of him, which tightens my grip on the oh-shit bar. "Maybe one of these days you'll begin to understand. When I'm driving, I flow *with* the world and not *against* it. Lights don't matter. Traffic doesn't matter. I'll never hit anybody because a crash would be imperfect. I'll never get a ticket because cops can't see what I'm doing as wrong."

We're close to my place now, in the land where no one parks on the street. Living around here means you're expected to provide ample off-street parking for yourself and your guests, however many that might include. But that's what you get when tech and VC money sit side-by-side with families whose wealth goes back to the gold rush.

My parents don't quite fit in among these estates. Some of our neighbors look down on us as "only" affluent.

Yeah, it gets kind of surreal around here.

But thinking of parking brings me to another question for Tony and his Zen and the Art of Speeding.

"How does your parking karma fit into this?"

"Don't dismiss a word like karma. It's more important than you think. And it should be obvious. Wherever I'm going, the perfect parking spot is always waiting because I'm always driving at the right time."

Tony's tires scream protests as he spins past the tall ash trees on the outer lawn and comes to a sudden stop on the cobblestones of my parents' circular driveway. Right in front of the house, perfectly parallel parked between two high-end Mercedes I don't recognize.

Two drivers who have never been here before, because they aren't using the huge parking garage off to the right. The one my parents converted from an old stable.

I lower the window and look down. Tony parked three inches from the curb, with no more than six inches between his bumpers and either of the two cars that cost multiple orders of magnitude more than his own.

I look back at Tony. He raises his eyebrows.

"I don't believe it," I say.

"And that is why you fail," he says. He doesn't even try for the Yoda voice. He leaves it implicit.

Reality shivers through me. "Sure you don't want to come in for a bit?"

"Sabrina and dinner will not wait. Besides, you have company."

That brings a moment of the old shared smile. He knows I want him to come in so I can avoid the company. I know he won't come in because my mom will trap him into playing host too. He's gotten almost as good at it as I have over the years.

But the smile doesn't last on my end. I still feel a pit of loss in my gut, stronger than I would have expected over Mary.

We say our goodbyes then, and I get out of the car. I consider crossing the huge, manicured lawn to the basketball court over by the garage for some free throw meditation, but Mom would just hear me dribble and call me in.

I could skip around the Korean lilac hedge and visit the Muellers. See how college went for Sara.

I sigh. That option could be fun. Except that my mom probably already told the Muellers I'm single again, in hopes of getting me a date with Sara. A date I wouldn't ask for, because I know I'm not Sara's type.

She wants guys who are as driven about their careers as she is about hers. I don't make the cut.

My options exhausted, I draw a deep breath and head up the shale walk for the heavy front door with its diamond-shaped window. The entrance to my parents' embarrassing three-story McMansion.

I PAUSE ON THE FRONT DOORSTEP, LETTING MY MIND RUN AHEAD OF ME through the door, past the entryway and into the living room.

Nothing.

No one in the living room, or the dining room, or the kitchen.

For the briefest moment I consider running my mind all through the house to find out just who all is here and where they are, but there's no need. The alarm is off.

Even though I can't remember the last time there was a break-in in our neighborhood, my parents have a state-of-the-art high-end alarm system. I suspect they only have it for the break on their home-owner's insurance, but they still use it religiously.

They don't leave the house or even go to bed without setting it, and since the code is six numbers long, I seriously doubt anyone could crack it without drawing attention.

So I know my parents are here somewhere. And I know they have guests...

And I know they aren't in the front part of the house.

I might be able to make it to my room without letting anyone know I'm here.

I ease open the heavy front door and slip inside the walnut entry-way, my shoes soundless on the plush maroon carpeting.

In the living room I see trays of hors d'oeuvres on both low coffee tables, partially picked over. No empty glasses though, and no coats or purses left on the leather sectional or either of the deep leather recliners.

The huge crystal chandelier dangling from the high ceiling is lit up for brightness, not mood lighting.

So this isn't a simple business meeting, or they would have gone straight to the office and not bothered with hors d'oeuvres. Could be new friends, but that's not likely because those Mercedes were parked out front. Dad likes to show off the garage to new friends.

That only leaves...

My head hangs forward.

Celebrities.

Great. Some actor or singer or athlete or something has decided to get involved with the Democratic Party, and has enough pull to get a meeting with people who really matter.

Don't get me wrong. I'm all for people getting involved in support of their political beliefs. It's just that when celebrities do it, I always feel like it's an angle. A half-informed publicity stunt or a desperate commitment to a cause they don't research enough to understand, rather than an attempt to do some good for our country.

Harsh, I know. But believe me, I've met a bunch of famous movie stars and pop idols and top athletes and there's no IQ test to succeed at their jobs. I'm not saying they're stupid. It's just that they aren't any smarter than anyone else. They just happen to have talent that gives them a really big soapbox to stand on when they talk about what they consider important.

And now Mom and Dad are — probably either in the back yard or the home theater — testing the waters with that celeb to see if their soapbox would be a help or a hindrance to the Democratic Party.

So much for sneaking away to my room.

If my mom finds out I was home and missed meeting So-and-So, she will feel obligated to arrange a chance for me to meet them. That's never not awkward, especially when it turns out to be someone I wouldn't want to meet anyway.

But I never have the heart to tell my mom no about these things. She holds the opinion that I've had to grow up too fast, playing proper guest and host for diplomats, stars, politicians and so on. So she never wants me to miss out on the perks she can get me, like occasional awesome Giants tickets, or the chance to meet famous people.

I sigh, then let my mind open up until I can feel the buzz of thoughts — my parents and four strangers, all out on the back lawn. Mom and Dad feel happy. This must be going well.

Time to find out.

I take off my Giants cap and put it on the top shelf of the coat closet behind me. This coat closet is for guests — empty right now — but if I put my cap here I know either I will remember it or Magda the maid will find it and put it back in my room.

The jersey I leave on. Might be a decent conversation starter. I'd rather talk baseball than politics right now.

And feeling as ready as I'm going to get, I start the walk down the long hallway filled with family pictures, and certificates of achievement from all three of us. No political pictures here. Those are either in the office or the upstairs hall.

I pass the kitchen, dining room, library and billiard room, then come to the glass door that leads out onto the patio.

I puff out a deep breath, and fix my "showtime" smile on my face. The one that's bright and says "I'm thrilled to be here," and suggests at least some warmth.

Yeah, I know. I only use it for these sorts of things. It makes me feel like a used car salesman.

Then I open the door and step out into whatever's waiting for me on the patio.

My parents' back yard is big enough to host a party for at least two hundred people. And has.

The manicured lawn itself is about the area of a football field, though some of that is taken up by the Olympic-sized swimming pool with attached Jacuzzi.

Out beyond the grass is what I like to think of as our forest. It's actually just a grove, but it's full of tall, thick redwoods — and one stump. My stump. A stump wide enough for me to lay across, but if I gave you the details about it right this second I would bore you to tears.

Besides, I'll probably go visit it soon enough.

Once we get rid of our guests, I'll probably go flop on my stump and contemplate what it means that we lost Mary. Right now I just have that heavy feeling in the pit of my stomach, and I feel as though I'm avoiding doing any serious thinking about it.

My stump is the perfect place for that kind of serious thinking.

But serious thinking will come later.

Between me and the yard and the forest beyond lies the patio. Half a basketball court of shale tiles blending three shades of blue into a pattern that might make sense if I could look down at it in a helicopter.

Six sets of fine, padded lawn furniture kept party-pristine for entertaining on very little notice, but only one set in use right now. The set over closest to the giant brick barbecue.

A grill big enough for two dozen steaks at once, where my dad is in his element. Wearing his barbecue apron over a jacketless suit and tie, he's flipping two burgers at once, with four more waiting their turns.

Not all those patties look quite like meat.

They smell like meat though, and my dad is using that blend of spices he came up with that always makes my stomach rumble, even when I'm not hungry.

All right, I'm a little hungry. Those garlic fries were more than two hours ago now, even though their taste lingers on my tongue.

Looks like I was right about four guests. Two middle-aged guys in suits, a big bald bruiser in all black except a navy blue blazer, and ... is that Isla Perkins? In a pale green sundress? She's got the willowy frame and the long blonde hair, but ... I don't know ... I had the impression she was the sort to dress in all the latest fashions all the time.

Just goes to show that even pop stars don't always live up to their image.

The guy in the blazer has already noticed me. Thoughts focused on threat assessment. I shift my smile to puzzled and inoffensive, but his thoughts don't shift in the least.

He already knows how he'd try to take me down if I did the wrong thing. Lovely.

My mom is telling some anecdote that has everyone laughing as I approach. From the edges of her thoughts — and believe me, even that is more of my mother's mind than I ever want to read — it feels like the musical limos story.

"...and then the German ambassador said to me — completely deadpan — 'all right, but when the music stops we have to get in whatever limousine is closest.'"

They all laugh — except the bodyguard — so I chuckle as I approach.

"There you are!" says my mom, who must have had some warning about Isla's outfit, because this is the first time this year that I can recall seeing her in something that doesn't have a designer label and a four-figure cost.

But my mom has the confidence to make any outfit work, even a eggshell-white pantsuit she might have gotten off the rack someplace. Another woman her size might look like an ostrich egg in that outfit, but Mom makes it look like something a First Lady would wear.

She handles the introductions with a flick of the wrist.

"Everyone, I'd like to present my son Rick, finally home from the Giants game. Rick, I'm sure you know that this is Isla Perkins, and over here we have her agent Bob O'Leary, her manager David Gold, and her driver, Hank Ross.

"Isla, Rick must have watched the video for your last single a hundred times."

Wow. Zero to totally embarrassed in one sentence. That's a record even for my mom. I'm now blushing hard enough that heat must be coming off me in waves.

After all, the single was catchy, but that wasn't the reason Tony and I watched the video...

Isla comes to my rescue.

"Tell me the Giants won. After the way the Dodgers beat up my Mets last week I want to see them go *down in flames*." Her face wrinkles up with vicious pleasure in those words the way only a true sports fan can understand.

And I admit, in that moment I forget I'm embarrassed. In fact, I forget about my parents, her agent, her manager, even her "driver." There's just her and me sharing a moment.

Damn, this girl's good. No wonder she's an international megastar.

I'm actually at ease again and smiling when I say, "Smacked them down eight to three. Knocked Kersey out of the box in the fourth."

"Yes," she says drawing out the word and pumping her fist. "Tell me all about it, Rick, and don't leave out a hit."

"We do have to be at the airport at seven," says ... I think it's her manager.

"We can arrange a later flight for you if you like," says my dad, handing out burgers, starting with Isla and my mom. They get the two patties that must be some kind of "healthy" vegetarian abomination.

"Isla has a photo shoot in New York at nine tomorrow morning."

"Don't talk about me like I'm not here." Isla takes a bite of her burger like she has all the time in the world.

"I'm just saying..." starts her manager, but Isla looks up at my dad.

"This is wonderful. What did you season it with?"

Dad just smiles and hands out more burgers, then throws a fresh patty on the grill for me.

"I've been trying to get him to tell me that for twenty years," says Mom.

"Did you inherit your father's culinary expertise, Rick?" says Isla, still ignoring her...

Manager. Yes. The sense of self pervading his fog of thoughts insists he's her manager. Gold.

"I'm all right, but—"

"Don't let him fool you," says Mom. "As often as we have to travel for our work, Rick has had to become a gourmet chef."

"Isla, I didn't mean—" starts Mr. Gold, but Isla cuts him off.

"I'll be rested and fresh-faced and smiling for the camera before the first shutter click. Now stop being rude to our hosts."

Mr. Gold wants so badly to stand up and yell "This isn't a party!" that I worry he's going to pop a blood vessel.

"Dave's right about one thing," says Mr. O'Leary, checking his watch. "We *should* get back on topic. I'm not sure political ads are right for your image."

Interesting. Mr. O'Leary may be talking about political ads, but he's worried about me. And the look he thinks he sees in Isla's eyes.

Terrence always insists that telepaths are more naturally attractive than regular people. I never paid that much attention, but it's true that Isla's eyes do flick back to me while other people are talking.

"And we would never ask you to do political ads," says Mom.

"We're not interested in having you endorse candidates," says Dad. "You've been outspoken from time to time about legislation coming up for vote. We just think that the Democratic Party could help you time and phrase your statements to maximize their effect..."

I tune out a bit as Mom and Dad go into their own kind of song and dance, interspersed with questions from Isla and her manager.

I wonder if this is a modification of a regular pitch my parents make, or if this meeting is less spontaneous than it looks.

I could find out, but that's not where my curiosity takes me. Tempted as I might be to poke around in the mind of the first celebrity I've met since I gained my telepathy, I'm more curious about her bodyguard.

This Mr. Ross shifted his focus away from me the moment I sat down. The moment it became clear that I was no threat (however Mr. O'Leary might disagree with that assessment). But his attention isn't all on the perimeter either. He's also concerned about...

Mr. O'Leary? Mr. Ross considers Isla's agent a potential threat?

Mr. Ross is keeping a sharp eye on the way the agent checks his watch, the words he uses when he speaks, the way he positions himself when he sits.

Now this is something worth looking into...

"Marvelous," says my mom, shaking Isla's hand. "It's settled. And I assure you, the Democratic Party won't do anything to draw attention to any agreements we've made today. No one need ever know about our arrangement."

"I still don't like it," says Mr. Gold. "Isla, this is your image you're playing with. If one word gets out—"

"It won't," says my dad, smiling as though the manager had been suggesting the sun would rise in the north. "We've done this many times before, and no one in the press has ever been the wiser."

"I can tell you this is the first *I've* ever heard about anything like this," I say, trying not to think about how sinister it all sounds. Secret political meetings to fine-tune speeches given by non-politicians?

"Well, then," says Isla, "I guess I'll just have to hope you can keep a secret for me, Rick."

"As long as I don't have to pretend I haven't met you. My friend Tony will lose his ... his mind."

"Well, if we're done here," says her agent, standing up, "we should get moving."

"Not so fast," says Isla, pointing off to the right at my mother's pride and joy — her garden. "I want to see the garden before I leave."

"Oh, that's perfect," says my mom. "Rick can show you the garden while Tom and I give David here the assurances he needs about our discretion."

"We really ought to be leaving," says Mr. O'Leary.

"What do you say, Rick," says Isla, smiling as she stands and offers me her arm. "Care to make your friend Tony jealous and go for a walk in the garden with me?"

I CAN'T BELIEVE I'M ARM-IN-ARM WITH ISLA PERKINS, GOING FOR A stroll in my mom's garden. The garden is a sculpted masterpiece of living floral arrangement. Roses, peonies, rhododendrons, six varieties of daisies and countless others I couldn't begin to name. Each sight and smell leading naturally from the previous and into the next.

Isla's pale green sundress is just right for the occasion. Like she's the beautiful blonde elf princess being escorted home.

My jeans and Giants jersey don't quite match.

At least we aren't holding hands. Then I couldn't hide the sweat on my palms. I mean, I don't usually get star struck. But then again, most stars don't flirt with me, and Isla's tone has been decidedly flirty.

But she probably just flirts with all the guys. It has to be good for her to leave everyone feeling special and important in her wake.

On the other hand, Terrence seems to have a point about telepaths being disproportionately good-looking...

Isla's about my height of five-nineish, which makes her very tall for a woman, though not WNBA tall. But her movements are smooth and graceful and make mine feel clunky. Like I'm about to trip over my own sneakers, and we're only halfway to the garden.

And she smells ever so subtly like freesia, apple blossom, raspberry, and ... something else. But I'm not willing to lean close enough to try to figure out what.

Me, I'm just hoping I don't smell too much like sweat and the garlic fries I can still taste.

Also, I can feel her bodyguard following us. I can't hear his shoes on the pebble path behind us, but I can feel his mind. Alert. Aware. Knows I'm not going to try anything, but ready to take me down in case I'm the one guy in a hundred who'd do something stupid.

"So what are you studying at Cal?" Isla asks.

"Getting my general ed stuff out of the way mostly, while I try to decide between Psychology and Sociology."

"What's the sticking point of the choice?" A moment of laser focus in her eyes and her mind.

"Whether I'll find it more productive to study individuals or groups."

Isla leans down to sniff a yellow rose.

"That's not a sticking point," she says, eyes closed and apparently entirely involved in the smell, though at least a third of her attention is on our conversation.

"That's a repetition of the situation. What do you want to do that makes it hard to choose?"

I try to puzzle through that while she comes back from the rapture of the rose. Her eyes find a small, fast-moving cloud.

"People are always asking me to make movies or appear on television sit-coms or dramas. I always decline." She shakes her head. "I play five instruments, but I almost never play any of them onstage or in videos. Why do you think that is?"

"Image?"

"Yes, but not the way most people mean. People think my face is my brand." She snorts and rolls her eyes. "My manager is one of them. But he's wrong. My music. My songs. My message. Those are my brand.

"If I play a role that isn't me, I distract people from the music. If I play an instrument, my skill at that instrument will call attention away from the music itself.

"Even the photo shoots are a necessary evil. I'd skip them if I could.

"This face," — she points to herself and flashes me her magazine smile — "will fade. But my songs are forever."

"I hadn't thought of it that way."

"Almost no one does." She looks me in the eye, and I'm struck by the green-and-gold blend of her irises.

"What about you, Rick? What do you want to leave behind in this world when your time comes?"

"There's..." — careful how you say this, Rick — "there's a segment of our population that's lost. Disconnected. Most people don't even know they exist. I want to bring them together. Help them."

Isla smiles, and it's not a magazine smile. Nothing flashy. It doesn't even show her teeth. Just a small, sincere raising of the corners of her mouth.

It's the most beautiful thing I've ever seen.

"I'd say you have your answer," she says.

"Sociology it is," I say, and without missing a beat she has us walking again.

One turn later we reach the center of the garden — the fountain. Two Greek statues of women pouring out never-ending jugs of water. Two Greek statues of women in diaphanous gowns that display far more than they cover.

All of a sudden I am *very* aware of just how close I am to Isla

Perkins.

"Quite a statue," she says, her head tilted just a little and one eyebrow raised, her eyes full of mirth.

And that's when I realize I'm blushing again. The first time this statue has made me blush in more than five years.

But then, the statue isn't the whole reason I'm blushing.

"Yes, my mother is very fond of it. She put the statue in first and designed the garden around it."

Isla releases my arm, then moves over to stand beside the statue, posing like one of the women.

"What do you think?"

"I think you're making fun of me."

She laughs and straightens up. "I wouldn't go *that* far, but maybe I am teasing you. Just a little bit."

There's something about her that seems so genuine. And I know it isn't faked, or that would be plain to me in the fog of her thoughts, even though I'm trying hard not to read her mind.

Something that makes me want to warn her.

"Listen," I say, "how long has your driver been working for you?"

She blinks fast at the change of subject. "Years now, why?"

How do I say this?

"He seems to me to be keeping a close eye on your agent."

"Oh, probably just because Bob is new, and my last agent was embezzling from me." She waves away my concerned look. "It was caught quickly and I got all my money back. But that's probably put Hank on guard."

"I don't think that's it. I think you should ask him about it."

"Okay," she says slowly, disbelief all through her aspect. "Sure. Never hurts to check."

I've blown the moment now, but I wasn't going to try to kiss her anyway. It's too soon, and my mouth still tastes like garlic fries.

Plus, she's Isla Freaking Perkins, and I'd say she's only been flirting to be nice, and maybe to amuse herself.

I'd say that except for one thing.

Isla is thinking about that kiss too.

4

Mom's insufferable after Isla leaves.

I'm sitting out on the back patio with Dad as the summer sun sets, just trying to enjoy my burger and catch him up on the game. But Mom brings back a salad bowl of mixed vegetables for me as an excuse to gush.

"Wasn't she *wonderful*? I was *certain* she would be your typical airheaded pop star. But oh, she was a sharp one, wasn't she, Rick?"

"Yes, Mom."

"Hardly needed her manager or agent for this meeting at all. Saw all the angles herself, and got *straight* to the heart of the matter. Which causes she would support financially, which ones she would also speak about publically, and which ones she wouldn't touch. Did you see, Rick?"

"I wasn't here for that part of the meeting, Mom."

"In fact, her manager and agent were really only important for scheduling. But I suppose someone has to handle those details for her so she can keep her mind on her music and on the causes that matter to her."

"Definitely not your typical don't-talk-to-me-about-business artist," says Dad. "Seems to have her head screwed on straight."

"Well," I say with my mouth half-full of burger, "she did fire her last agent for embezzling."

"She told you that?"

Up until that question, Mom's surface thoughts had been whirling at high speed the way they always do after a big meeting. She's scary smart that way. Mom can talk ten miles a minute about one subject while her mind spins a hundred times as fast about more important matters.

But when Mom asks that question, it's like an all-stop for her mind.

And every ounce of that formidable brain is focused on me.

Don't get me wrong. Dad's just as smart. But Dad's got a subtlety to his approach that makes him less immediately intimidating and more long-term frightening.

Mom asks four simple words, and all of a sudden I'm reminded exactly how my parents got where they are today, doing what they do.

I swallow.

"Well, I told her I thought her driver was keeping a close eye on her agent."

"I didn't notice that," says Mom. "Did you, Dear?"

The barest flick of a head-shake from Dad.

"But *you* did." Mom smiles like her baby bird has started flying on his own. "Oh, are you *sure* you don't want an internship, Rick? With your perceptivity—"

"Sociology, Mom." I hold up a forestalling hand. "Unless I find out I hate it. Then we'll talk about politics."

"So you've decided between Psychology and Sociology?"

Dad looks at Mom, and a moment passes between them that isn't *quite* telepathic, but close enough that I wonder a little. It's almost like their fogs of thoughts touch.

Mom continues his line of thought.

"But just this morning you were talking about how hard the choice was."

"Almost as though someone helped you decide."

"Someone with a good handle on her own career. A good head for business."

"Someone very pretty."

"Guys, give me a break," I manage, but I know it's too late for what comes next out of Mom's mouth.

"And young Ms. Perkins did seem awfully taken with you."

"'Smitten' might be the word," adds Dad.

"And who could blame her," says Mom, growing more pensive as she considers the possibilities. "She has something of a public dating history though, doesn't she?"

"Mom, Dad, I love you both and I'm going inside now."

I leave them debating the relative merits of Isla Perkins as a possible girlfriend for me. Which just goes to show how truly surreal my life has become.

Today I met Hyun-Ki Noh, and not only is he a telepath, he acts as though he knows others. This could be terrific.

Today I found out Mary's dead.

Today I got to flirt with Isla Freaking Perkins.

One day. This has all been one day.

And the sun is only now finished setting.

I can't quite absorb it all. I've got a giddiness trying to force at least half a smile on my face, but a sense of loss in the pit of my stomach that makes me feel guilty for enjoying that little flirtation.

Which is all that probably was, Mom. Sorry to break it to you. I'm pretty sure Isla Perkins has romantic standards I don't meet.

Even if she did think about kissing me.

This is too much for me right now. I feel like my head's about to explode trying to deal with it all. Make some sense of it. Prioritize all the conflicting emotions.

Screw heading for my room. I don't even need my stump. Not now. I close the sliding glass door before it's half open and turn to walk around the side of the house toward the basketball court.

I need to meditate.

OUR BASKETBALL HALF-COURT IS OUT BEHIND THE CONVERTED STABLE / parking garage. Mom and Dad have already warned me that they're going to turn it into a tennis court after I graduate from Cal.

I'll miss it, but I can't blame them. I won't be here enough to get much use out of it, and I'm sure the tennis court would be appreciated by the kind of guests they entertain.

They probably won't have to change the surface too much. I'm not sure what this court is made out of, but it's a lot easier on the knees than the asphalt I find on most public courts. It's got the same kind of black look though, except for the key which is dark blue.

I'll miss our red-white-and-blue nylon net though. The public courts all use chain or white nylon. And the indoor courts, of course, are all white nylon. I don't think anyone else has used red-white-and-blue nets since the bicentennial, way back before I was born.

I've certainly never seen them anywhere else. Dad has them shipped to us special as his private tribute to the defunct American Basketball Association and his all-time favorite player, Dr. J. From what Dad tells me, Dr. J was the LeBron James of the Seventies.

The floodlights on this part of the property are activated by motion sensors, so with the sun mostly set now, the moment I step onto the court the evening flares from early twilight to full mid-day glow.

I dig out a ball from the hard plastic storage locker behind the basket. Also red, white and blue, but the tricolor basketballs aren't nearly as rare. I also dig out a ball-returner, and hook it onto the hoop so I can keep my mind on the process and not the result.

I bounce the ball a few times to test its inflation, then, satisfied with its response, dribble out to the free throw line.

And then I throw my complete focus into the individual steps of my routine.

I close my eyes, purse my lips, and push all the air out of my lungs and diaphragm until I have to curl forward a bit to finish. I slowly draw breath back into my body.

I flick my eyes to the basket then back to the ball. Spin the ball twice in my hands, bounce it three times with my right hand, my shooting hand. Bend my knees and back, not a lot, just enough to shorten my height by three or four inches. Eye flick. Spin the ball twice. Bounce three times. Spin twice. Eyes on the basket now. Spin the ball once more. Let my breath out.

Shoot, feet coming up on their toes but never leaving the ground, arms full extension.

The ball arcs up, comes down through the net with a breathy "pwuh" sound.

Tony's words come back to me unbidden. His instructions for free throw meditation.

"Shoot at least one hundred free throws, paying close attention to every step of your routine on every shot. You need to dig so far into what you're doing that you forget I'm here. That you forget anything else. Everything else. Nothing should exist for you except the ball and the basket.

"And shoot."

And that's what I do. The count is a trick. If I know how many free throws I've shot, then I'm doing it wrong. If I think about makes or misses, then I'm doing it wrong. If I worry about where the ball goes, then I'm doing it wrong.

Same pattern every time.

During my first shots I'm aware of the pattern. Of the basket. Of the rustle of the wind. The smell of hydrangeas from around behind the garage.

But my body is following the steps, the way it would if I were in a game. Trying to free my mind to focus on the basket. On making the shot.

I force my attention on each step in turn. Every bounce. Every spin. Every flick of my eyes.

I focus on the pattern until I become the pattern.

And once I am the pattern, then everything else fades to silence.

The wind and the hydrangeas. The taste of Dad's hamburger. The Giants game.

Isla Perkins flirting.

Finally, Mary's death.

All of them drift away until I am an empty vessel.

And I hold that state as long as I can.

Until there's a knock on my mind.

CLANG!

My shot — or should I say my brick — ricochets off the right edge of the hoop and heads for the lawn.

The sky is night black above me, and I can hear frogs proclaiming their love of my mom's garden. A slight evening chill I hadn't noticed shivers through me, and my legs complain at the movement as I trot after the ball.

I recognize the knock when it comes again. Jamal.

I open to contact as I collect the ball.

What the heck were you doing? It was like your mind was there and not there. I could tell where it was — at least enough to knock — but I couldn't get any sense of you or what you were doing.

—*Hi Jamal.*— I pick up the ball and dribble it back to the storage locker. —*I'm fine. How are you doing this evening?*—

Heh. I can feel the apology in his undertone. *Sorry about that. You know I get carried away by this shit.*

—*Fair enough. I was meditating.*—

So that's why you're so good at free throws.

—*Interview me for your research later, huh? It's been a long, weird day.*—

And it's about to get longer and weirder. I need you to join me for a deep chat.

I spin the ball in my hands and sigh. I'm fine with calling the meditation there. I've obviously been at it for a while, and I feel calm and centered again. Almost calm and centered enough to try to put some serious thought into the events of the day.

Almost.

—*Is it important? I'm really kind of beat. And I have to make a phone call.*—

There's no way Tony would forgive me for not telling him I met Isla Perkins. He's a huge fan. Of her looks, anyway.

It's important, he responds and his undertone carries his confident nod. *Now do you want me to take real time convincing you of that? Or do you want to trust me and get the whole situation in less time than it would take me to explain it?*

—*Fine. Be right there.*—

I sigh again and reach for Jamal's mind. It's a simple process — focusing on my sense of Jamal until his mind feels clear in my head. Then I just stretch out toward that sense of him and

---

I'M STANDING INSIDE THE FRONT DOOR OF A DINER. OLD, 50S STYLE, complete with a line of red vinyl booths. Jamal sits in the back corner booth. The window wall is all black beyond, even the glass door I just came through.

Behind the counter fusses a woman in late middle age. She looks vaguely familiar in her pink uniform, like I've seen her on television. The place is clean but not spotless, and smells like bacon and eggs with an undercurrent of burnt coffee.

A small pot of coffee sits on our white Formica table, next to the napkin dispenser. A cup for him, complete with dish and stirring spoon, but not for me. Little jugs of cream and milk look out of place next to the crusty sugar dispenser, but I let it go.

Instead of coffee, a tall lemon-lime fizz sits in front of my seat.

Jamal lounges in the corner, his back against the window and his legs up on the seat.

"I couldn't remember how you like your coffee. I hope the fizz works for you."

"That's because I don't drink coffee. But just about anything lemon-lime will work for me." The seat hisses air as I drop onto it. "So what's going on?"

"I went to check ton Pete and Repeat. Mary had them assigned to different partners to help their recovery, but—"

"Wait. Why would that help?"

"Everything they did for her, they did together. So the more time apart, the better."

I shudder as I try not to think of what all Mary had them do together.

"May I continue?"

Jamal has that long-suffering look on his face, as though I'd committed the height of rudeness by asking a question. I know he's joking though, or I'd remind him of who is interrupting whose evening.

I swirl tiny circles with my right hand to gesture for him to go on.

"Anyway, I started with Pete LeMaster because he's married."

"I'm surprised Mary bothered with a married man. She could have found one who was single. Saved herself the extra effort."

"If you would listen," says Jamal with a sigh, "you would know that Pete was already a three-time cheater. No extra groundwork needed."

I start to say something, but Jamal hurries on ahead so I take a sip of the fizz instead. Pure, sweet lemon-lime goodness.

"Anyway, I've been doing more work on Pete because I don't want his wife to suffer more than she has to through all of this."

Jamal arches an eyebrow as he sips some coffee. Daring me to interrupt again. I smile, but settle for another taste of my fizz.

"His recovery is coming along fine. His dreams are settling down, and his misunderstood urges to go to a certain apartment building are fading. Even without any more help from us, his mind should be fully his own again in no more than six months."

I find myself wondering about the way his mind is recovering. Mary set some pretty heavy controls in the man's mind, but even Mary would have worked with what was there first. Easier to sculpt from a pre-cut block than to first chip that block out of a boulder.

"But that's not the part I wanted to talk to you about." Jamal narrows his eyes at me, no doubt sensing that my thoughts have wandered. He sighs. "Fine. If you have any questions about his recovery, ask them now and get them out of the way."

"Nothing pressing." I shake my head. "Honest. We should talk about this, but you said there was something important."

"And there is. I just don't want to be interrupted."

I sip from my fizz.

"Good," he says. He takes one more drink of coffee, then sets down the cup and leans forward, his feet on the floor now. "Kelly's been checking up on him. No mental traces or anything. No reason to believe Kelly's gotten his powers back or anything. But still, Pete has seen Kelly three times during his patrols this week.

"And I don't just mean he's seen him. Kelly's been talking to him. Asking questions. Innocent ones right now, but I think he's working up to something."

"That doesn't sound like Kelly. That sounds like Stephen. You think they're still hanging out?"

"Probably. Stephen likes having underlings, and even without his scanning Stephen's stronger personality would keep Kelly in line. Don't underestimate Kelly, though. He might not be top of the class, but he's smart enough to hold his own in a science major at Cal, and he's motivated to get back at us."

"At me, you mean."

"No, I burned the bridge for the rest of us when I told him we agreed with what you did." Jamal shrugs. "Yeah, you didn't ask us first, but what's the point of forming a community if it isn't all for one and one for—"

Sharp, intense pain in my chest. My heart. Body shaking.

Another. My head this time. My

5

____

No.

I'm back in my body now. In my own head. I'm still standing on the basketball court at my parents' house. It's still night. Croaking frogs. Chilly breeze. Lemon-lime fizz taste fades to traces of Dad's hamburger.

And my body and head. Intact.

Ghost pain in my head and heart. Fading.

Not my body and head then.

Jamal.

I reach for his mind again.

Nothing.

Think, Rick. Think think think.

I've been to his apartment. I know where that is. I stretch for my memory of his Berkeley place. Two bedrooms, rent control. Decorated in the same smooth style as he dresses. The apartment he wants to leave me as a legacy when he moves out in August.

No minds in that apartment.

—*JAMAL!*— Loud as I can make it. Everything I can put in one burst.

Nothing.

I'm on my knees on the court now. Hot tears on my face.

No. No reason to cry yet. Stop it. You don't know.

Not dreaming. I could reach him dreaming.

Not unconscious. Jamal and I made contact with Stephen when he was in a coma.

Well, we went into his mind, anyway.

Not a coma.

I try again.

Nothing.

Like there's no Jamal to reach.

The sob erupts from my chest before I can stop it.

—Terrence!—

Imprecise sending, but I know his mind well enough to reach him anyway.

You sound awful, what...

—Jamal. I think he's dead.—

Why...

I don't wait for the question. I send him the whole conversation the quick way. My memory of the experience.

You asshole!

—I think he's dead, Terrence.—

*If you **ever** send me something like that again... Without warning...*

—I said—

And I heard you. And you better hear me.

I try to focus on my breathing while I give Terrence a moment to recover from the sudden shock. But a moment is all I can give him.

—I'm sorry. I should have at least warned you. But—

I know. You think he's dead. And I think you're right.

—You're the one with police contacts. Can you do anything? Maybe he's—

Rick, I'm in L.A., and my contacts are in Oakland, not Berkeley. And neither of us knows where he was when it happened. So, no.

—But we have to—

Watch the police reports. Look for a shooting. Gangland style.

—Oh, come on. Jamal wasn't—

One to the heart. One to the head. Gangland style.

—Assassination?—

I'll try to make contact with guys I know on the force. Maybe they'll hear something.

—Right.— One more deep breath. *—Right. I'll see what I can dig up too.—*

Good. I'll make contact at midnight so we can compare notes.

—Watch yourself, Terrence. If that was a gangland style hit, then it wasn't some mugger who shot Mary.—

—Someone might be coming after our group. Which means one of us is next.—

INTERLUDE ONE

Transcription of a phone call between Rick Blackhall and Tony Gottschalk.

Rick: It's not just Mary. Jamal's dead.

Tony: Holy shit. Hang on.

The sounds of murmured apologies and shuffling, then hurried padded steps.

Tony: Go.

Rick: I was in touch with his mind. He was talking about Pete's recovery—

Tony: Pete?

Rick: Of Pete and Repeat fame.

Tony: Right. Go on.

Rick: We were having one of those deep talks that take no time. Just bullshitting in that Fifties diner he loved so much. Then ... I felt it. The pain. Fear. Panic. Heart and head. Then nothing. (Rick sobs) Nothing at all.

Tony: Heart. And head.

Rick: Yeah, that's what Terrence said. Gangland style.

Tony: We need to get you out of town.

Rick: No. I need to know what's going on. I need to—

Tony: You *need* to get your ass out of town. As in yesterday. Go visit Jenna in Montana or something. But you need to clear the fuck out.

Rick: I can't just—

Tony: Two of you are dead in the space of a day. One a "mugging," but one a flat out execution. Montana might not be far enough. How about we go to Germany? You and me. I've got relatives—

Rick: Oh, so I should not only run, I should put you and your family in danger?

Tony: What do you know about fighting assassins?

Rick: WHAT DO I KNOW ABOUT RUNNING FROM ASSAS-SINS? I'm better off staying here where I know the area. I'll just start paying closer attention to—

Tony: Look, I know you've got your "knack" and all, but you always said Jamal was good. Maybe better than you.

Rick: Moot point now.

Tony: If they got the drop on him someplace he felt comfortable, what makes you think they can't get to you?

Rick: Shit. I've got to go. My dad's knocking.

6

———

I force out a yawn as I open the door to my room. As expected, my dad is standing there, hand poised to knock again if needed.

As not expected, my dad's mind feels worried. Worse, it's a collected kind of worried that says he took a moment to muster his forces before coming to talk to me.

"You know..." he says with that slight lift to his right eyebrow I know so well. It's the look he used to give me when he already knew what I was guilty of, but he was going to question me anyway to test my honesty. "On almost any day of the year, if I heard you use the word 'assassin' I would assume it had something to do with a video game.

"But I know you just a little bit better than that, Rick. Ever since you took up this meditation-by-free-throws of yours, you've come in from shooting calm, cool, and collected. Smiling.

"Tonight you came in trying to hide the fact that you'd been crying and you rushed straight to your room. Now I can tell you that no public figures have been assassinated this week, but something has you spooked and panicking. So you tell me. What's going on?"

"I..." I slump against the door frame. "After I got finished meditating, I got a phone call. A good friend of mine from school is dead."

"Do you want to talk about it?"

No, Dad. I don't want to talk about it. I want it to not be true. I want it to be Jamal testing some sort of new technique. Something he could share with me in an attempt to get me to let him read my mind while I'm meditating.

I don't want it to be true that Mary's dead either. I especially don't want it to be true that they're both dead.

But they are. Even without confirmation on Jamal, I know it. I've never before been so completely unable to find a mind I know well.

But I can no more reach Jamal than I can reach Mary.

And that's not all, Dad. Chances are that a killer is coming for your only son. Because I'm a telepath.

I don't want to talk about any of this, Dad. I don't want it to be true. I just want to cry myself to sleep and have Terrence contact me at midnight to tell me that Jamal's not dead. That he was hit by some kind of special tranq and that we have to go rescue him.

Because even that would be better.

I don't want to face any of this, Dad. And I sure don't want to tell you about it. I don't want you to worry. I don't want you to face the truth about your son. What that truth might mean for your son's future. Assuming he — assuming I — even have a future.

But I see that patient look in my dad's eyes. Eyes that look so like my own in the mirror. Eyes that say he wants to hear it, and whatever it is he'll help if he can.

I see that look and I know I can't lie to him.

"No, Dad, I don't want to talk about it. But I think I have to."

Dad offers to sit with me in his office so we can talk privately, man to man. But that's not enough for this. If I'm going to tell my dad, tell my parents, what's going on, it has to be both of them.

And I sure as hell don't want to do it twice.

So we go down to the living room, where Mom and Dad sit together on the leather sectional. Holding hands, apprehensive, like newlyweds at the doctor's office finding out whether or not they'll ever be able to have children.

I have to bite my tongue to pull back from the apprehension in the room. My stomach is doing flip-flops anyway. This is the wrong day for this conversation. Too much on top of everything else.

"Rick..." My mom. Worried about my silence. My closed eyes.

But I need another moment to shove as much of my attention as I can into the feel of my jeans and the places they rub against my thighs as I sit. The sensations of my athletic socks against the soles of my feet, soft but just rough enough that I can't unnotice it once I feel it.

Good.

"To understand this, you need to understand it all."

Another wave of anxiety pushes out from them. I scrape my fingernails against my palm to keep it from dragging me under.

My breath comes faster now. My pulse pounds in my throat.

"That coma last year. It was my brain shutting down my body while it tried to acclimate to a new sense awakening. I'm a telepath."

Confusion pushes past the anxiety, and the momentary relief makes me shiver and sigh.

"Don't say anything yet. You have to let me tell it."

And I do. I tell them all about my struggle to stop picking up every single stray and casual thought that came anywhere near me. That overwhelmed me and drove me to the brink of suicide before I took a cue from the animals of the forest and learned to focus my attention and avoid caring about anything that didn't matter.

If only the stress and anxiety of my parents — about their son, no less — could be ignored so easily.

I tell them how I gained control, and how I exacted my revenge on the bully Andre Valchek. The awful regret I felt and my efforts to make amends. The rules system Tony and I came up with.

(I consider leaving Tony out of it, but I know my parents would feel better knowing I wasn't dealing with this all on my own.)

I tell them of my freshman year and the other telepaths I met (naming only the deceased). The abuses others indulged in and the clash I led to stop those abuses.

I even tell them how the girlfriend they met over winter break — Amaris — was set up for me by another telepath, and how I struggled with what that meant and how I could make sure I wasn't taking unfair advantage of her.

That gets a wave of relief from Mom that almost makes me laugh. Guess she didn't really like Amaris. Probably didn't approve of her Apex Goth style.

Then I get to today, and how I learned about the "mugging" that took Mary's life. And how I had been in touch with Jamal...

"So you think they were assassinated because of their ... telepathy?"

Dad's trying hard to believe, but it's tough.

"Telepathy is how I knew Isla's bodyguard doesn't trust her agent. And..." — I squeeze my eyes shut as I admit this next part — "...it's the reason Kersey struggled against the Giants today. That was me."

"Did you read Isla's mind too?" Casual words, but Mom's mind is whirling a thousand miles an hour as usual.

"No. I pick up a lot of stuff casually. Things people think loudly without knowing they're doing it." Like Isla's imagining kissing me. "But I don't go skimming through everyone's internal monologue all the time. And in a one-on-one moment like that walk with Isla? I fought to keep away from her mind."

"So are you reading our thoughts right now?"

"I've worked like hell to never read your guys' minds at all. Sometimes I notice if you're thinking about me or Tony, and right now your stress and anxiety is driving me nuts. But no, I'm not reading your minds."

"That's why the free throws," says Dad, quietly making connections in his head.

"Tony's idea. The meditation really helps daily life." I run both hands through my hair, mixing forehead sweat with palm sweat in the process. "In fact, I want to go shoot more right now."

"You know we have to call the police," says Mom.

"Not just the police." Dad looks at Mom and she nods, a small movement that tempts me more to read their minds than anything ever has.

"What do you want to tell them?" I say. "Mary's death looks like a mugging gone wrong, and Jamal. I don't even know if they've found a body."

"We can tell the police you've gotten a death threat," says Dad. "And anyone with a family in politics has to take those seriously."

"And what about those other people you want to call?"

"The local police might not be up to handling this."

"Forget it." I hop to my feet. "The Feds are never finding out that I can read minds. I will *vanish* before I let them make me a lab rat."

"Sit down, Rick," says my dad, in that tone that has me sitting before I know I've done it. His voice is quiet now, and forceful. And Mom is letting him lead the conversation even though I can tell she would say all the same things herself.

"If you think, for even one moment, that your mother and I would let anyone take you away and make you a lab rat—"

"It's not—"

"Did I tell you to speak?"

"No, sir."

My dad's presence has filled the room. Calm and terrible. Fury in suspension.

"Don't you forget who we are. Your mother and I started with nothing but the work ethic your grandparents inspired. We built our careers without family money and without patrons watching over us. And no one rises from nothing to get this high up in politics without making connections.

"We have friends. Friends who will pull strings when they find out our only boy's life is in danger.

"No one needs to know about your special talent. They only need to know that there have been two deaths the local police don't have the information to connect, and that those deaths make you a target."

"But there's no connection between us except telepathy. It's not like we're a study group or—"

"Or a club?" says Mom. "Why would anyone think you were a club? You only met once a week on campus for a whole semester. Isn't that what you said?"

My jaw drops. The four of us met so often in our heads I had forgotten that we met in person at least once a week, and even started getting together socially.

"So we tell them it's a game club of some sort," says my father, his voice more back to normal, "and leave the details out."

"Do you think that will work?" I say.

"Better than you running off on your own. You're a bright boy, son, and this talent of yours give you an advantage no one could prepare for. But if someone's been hired to kill you, you need professional protection."

I hate the idea of more people getting involved. And not just because more people could die, though that's part of it. The risk of strangers finding out about me. Especially of government agents finding out about me. Of more people knowing what I am.

That's pretty scary.

But I don't see any alternatives.

I NEED ANOTHER HALF-HOUR OF FREE THROWS TO GET MY HEAD BACK under control. I set a timer on my watch to make sure I don't just stay at it for the rest of the night.

But the timer goes off, and I stop mid-routine. That would drive Tony nuts. He would tell me to finish the shot, then stop. But as far as I'm concerned, the alarm is my stop sign, and I don't have any more time to waste.

I put away the ball and returner, then head back inside and to my room. I can't hear my parents as I move through the halls and up the stairs, but I can feel them all the same. In their respective offices. On the phone, no doubt.

My parents' master suite is at one end of the hall, and my bedroom is at the other. In between there's the family museum —

storehouse of photos, awards, childhood drawings and all the other things that sane families pack away in storage — the two guest bedrooms that share a common full bath, the guest room that has to use the hall bath, and finally my room at the far end.

My room's the only one in the whole house that would end up on the cutting room floor if *Better Homes and Gardens* ever did a shoot of our place. Oh, I've got the same high-end dark wood look, from the frame of my queen-sized bed to my two — yes, two — nightstands, and my huge bureau. And on this floor we all have the same plush, forest-green carpeting that's soft enough to fall asleep on.

All that would probably be fine, if not for the trio of Three Coyotes tour posters, the signed photograph of Janette "The Black Widow" Lee, and my stills from the *Evil Dead* trilogy.

But none of that is on my mind as I grab my laptop off my desk and flop on the bed. All I care about right now is finding out what happened to Jamal.

Ten minutes later I've read unhelpful news headlines about the young African American male shot dead with a high-powered rifle.

All the local papers and news sites are speculating gang involvement. None of them seem to have any idea who Jamal was. Or care.

Don't these idiots realize that Jamal never went near any of that crap? Don't they know he graduated with a straight-A average in Psychology? That he had a summer internship in phase one of a study about the unintended consequences of frequent exposure to neurolinguistic programming techniques? That he had a fellowship covering every dollar of the Ph.D. program he was due to start this fall?

That he had a girlfriend in the Economics department?

Oh, God. Suzi doesn't know.

My guts start wringing me like a wet towel. Tears dripping down my cheeks again. Heavy, deep pain in my belly and head. Heat, all through my face and neck.

Any benefit I got from that last round of free throws gets wrung out with the tears.

I lose time just crying. Who could be doing this to us? Why would anyone do this to us?

Why would anyone kill Jamal?

I hate myself for admitting it, but Mary I kind of understand. She had a casual cruelty to her. The sort of person who could and did twist men to her liking. Yeah, she'd been improving, but that was after months or years of being the way she was. That someone could have hated her from high school enough to snap one day and come after her, that didn't seem a huge stretch to me.

Of course, Jamal wasn't a saint either. In moments of weakness he seduced the girlfriends of obnoxious racist assholes. Girlfriends who secretly longed to have what they claimed they feared. One of those boyfriends might have...

I smack myself in the forehead.

What the hell am I doing?

Blaming Jamal? Blaming Mary? Both had their bad points, but nothing worth shooting them over. They're the victims here.

And Terrence or me could be next.

This kind of crying and struggling is exhausting. I'm fatigued to the point of dead arms and heavy eyelids. I long to put my head down and sleep.

But I focus on my breathing and keep reading websites. I force myself to stop thinking about the fact of Jamal's death and try to learn the facts around it.

High-powered rifle. Two shots. Eight-twenty in the evening. He was on campus. Lower Sproul Plaza, in the outdoor seating area of the Bear's Lair Pub. Plenty of witnesses, but no one who knew him.

Check that. This one has a girl arriving after campus police were on the scene. A girl who saw the body and went into hysterics.

Suzi knows then. Poor thing. I should...

Stay on point, Rick.

So Jamal was at the Bear's Lair to meet Suzi. Having a beer. Made contact to catch me up. Got shot. Twice.

Is that significant?

Did the killer wait until Jamal made contact with me?

I don't see how he could have known. How anyone could have known. Deep conversation takes almost no time. The killer would have had to have Jamal in his sights already. Been watching for some sign...

Jamal must have looked into the distance. Or closed his eyes. Something. Something that would have been a clue to someone who was watching for it. A clue that his mind was occupied.

That he was too busy to sense the danger. That he was vulnerable.

So there's no doubt then. The killings must be related. And the killer knows we're telepaths.

Fear tries to work its way up my spine, but I'm just too exhausted to feel more than a vague flutter.

I try another search phrase and keep reading.

TERRENCE DOESN'T USUALLY GO FOR DEEP CONTACT. HE CONSIDERS IT too intimate. Too much potential for either or both people finding out way more than they ever meant to.

I would argue the point, except that the last time someone tried to kill me — or at least kill my personality and make me his slave — it all started during a deep conversation.

And just in fighting my way free I learned more about that freaky bastard Stephen's past than I ever wanted to know.

Well, I didn't just fight my way free. But that's not the point.

The point is that Terrence inviting me to make deep contact at midnight was unexpected, and probably would have been a little concerning if my concern meter weren't already pegged out right now.

But right now I'm sitting in his image of Sufficient Grounds, the coffee shop in Berkeley where he and I would sometimes meet to talk. It has the baked goods and roast coffee smell I know well.

But unlike the real café, this one is empty. Every table, big or small. And no one's behind the counter, serving up fresh pastries or sandwiches or fifteen kinds of coffee or tea or smoothies.

Terrence is sitting at his usual little square table in the back, in his usual faded Dodgers tee shirt and jeans, with his usual cup of coffee on the table in front of him.

Before I take my hard, wooden seat I can tell the drink is my favorite green tea smoothie with blackberry and honey.

"The police leaked the gang story, to give the papers something to chew on. But they know better. He had ID on him for Christ's sake. It wasn't hard to find out who he was and after Suzi showed up, what he was doing there."

Terrence doesn't seem at all interested in his fake coffee or the pretense of sitting where he appears to be sitting. He just keeps talking.

"What they don't know is why anyone would come after him with a high-powered rifle. They can't even claim it was a typical school shooting, because the killer stopped with Jamal. Two quick shots, and gone. No trace so far. Not even any certainty of where the shots were fired from."

"But I thought modern ballistics—"

"He spun as he fell, and no one paid enough attention to say for sure which way he'd been facing. That means that the killer could have been shooting from any one of five or six vantage points. They may know over time but they don't know yet."

"Who's handling the investigation?" I pick up my smoothie. The taste might help right now.

"That's under dispute too. The city wants it, but the campus is claiming jurisdiction."

I drop the smoothie. It starts to tip over, then rights itself.

"They're going to bury this, aren't they?"

"Tough to say," he says with a sigh. Hard to tell from his personal image profile, but Terrence looks almost as tired as I feel.

"But if I had to bet, that's the way I'd go. They can't bury it completely, but they're going to downplay it as much as they can to avoid the effect it could have on this fall's incoming class."

I catch Terrence up on my own findings and theories.

"I hate to say it but I think you're right. Someone's after telepaths, and we're on the list."

"So what do we do? How do we stop him?"

"Simple." Terrence picks up his coffee and drains it in a single go. "We vanish. No one can do that like we can. You go your way, and I'll go mine."

"You just want to ... what? Run for the rest of your life?"

"Running and living longer beats staying and dying sooner."

Terrence stands up. Without words he gives me the sense that it's time to go.

I hang in right where I am.

"So what about the BTO?"

"It's dead. Gone with Jamal and Mary. You and I are now just telepaths who happen to know each other."

"I don't accept that. We've been working so hard to—"

"Fine." The word comes out clipped, but the undercurrent is pure exasperation. "Tell you what. Wherever we are in the world, we'll try to make contact at twenty-three-fifty-nine GMT on the first night of each month. If we go three months failing to make contact because of distance or death, we give it up and either see each other somewhere down the line or in heaven, whichever comes first."

"But, Terrence, together we could—"

"Goodbye, Rick. I'll see you when I see you."

AND JUST LIKE THAT, I'M BACK IN MY OWN HEAD, WHICH IS IN MY bedroom, on my pillow.

So that's it then. The Berkeley Telepathic Outreach is done. Even if we both survive the assassin, I doubt Terrence will be willing to form another group.

My dreams of forming a community of telepaths. As dead as Jamal and Mary.

This isn't the time to worry about that though.

In fact, if Hyun-Ki tries to make contact with me, I should probably put him off for now.

Hyun-Ki...

Now, Hyun-Ki is a telepath I met today. He spotted me before I spotted him. If he hadn't made contact, I might not have known he was there.

But he *is* a telepath. And he clearly recognizes telepaths easily enough, and just as clearly is in contact with other telepaths.

What if he's behind — or at least affiliated with — the assassinations?

He was at the game, but said he didn't like baseball. He was there "entertaining a client" but he didn't say who the client was or what he did for a living.

Was the entertainment the baseball game? Or the telepath interfering with the baseball game?

In my attempt to have a little fun, did I inadvertently trigger our...

No. Wait. Too much information in one day. I'm getting it all confused.

Mary wasn't shot today. She was already dead before I started messing with the game.

That doesn't mean Mr. Hyun-Ki Noh is innocent. It just means that I didn't trigger anything.

At least, not today.

All right. Stop right there, Rick. What else do you know?

I reach out to Darcy's mind, as though to make contact. I can feel her thoughts before I come close enough to "knock." I almost back off there, satisfied in the knowledge that she, at least, is still alive.

But I knock anyway.

You feel troubled, Rick. And exhausted. Spent. What's going on?

Darcy's thoughts are smooth, gentle. Sympathetic. Just distant enough to hold back opinion while bringing across some concern.

—Someone killed Mary. Made it look like a mugging so we didn't suspect anything. But now they've killed Jamal. I think they're coming for the rest of us, but that might not include you.—

If it didn't, it does now. What do you need?

—I thought you didn't want to join—

My unwillingness to be a mere citizen when I could be a queen does not mean I will stand by and let someone murder my friends.

Darcy sees us as her friends? I knew she tolerated us, but I had no idea...

Honestly, Rick, when you get tired you leak like a sieve. Mary could have died screaming in a fire and I would not have lost a wink of sleep. Why the rest of you tolerated her I don't pretend to know, but I would like to think it wasn't just her bust size.

—We're so few in number—

Yes, yes, that was ever your credo and Jamal's as well. My point is that while I would not have spared a single thought to save Mary, I would not see you, Jamal or Terrence dead. I may be too late to help Jamal, but...

—Terrence is going to vanish. Make contact once a month until he accepts that we're safe.—

Then he is a fool. Life is unsafe by definition. I can feel your concerns and conflicts. Work them through. And when you are ready to hunt Jamal's killer and make him pay, contact me. I will give you whatever help you need.

Darcy cuts the connection at that point, but it's just as well. I'm too tired to even parse though all of what she had to say, as fast as it was coming out of her.

The point is, I still have at least one telepathic ally I can call on if worse should come to worse.

Or if I find out that Hyun-Ki is behind all of this. Or even affiliated with it.

I don't know Mr. Noh well. He might be telepath enough to stand against just me. He might even be good enough to stand against Darcy.

But against us both? Good luck.

7

I'M DREAMING. SOMETHING ABOUT ISLA PERKINS COMMANDING A LEGION of faceless NSA agents who take down the assassin, but then have to take me into protective governmental custody "for my own good."

Isla tells me that as we're sitting in an interrogation room. The moment feels both sexy and scary. But Tony's Rambler Storm Warning bursts through the solid iron wall. "Time to Run Amok" by the Cold Skankin' Boys blasts on his stereo.

"Come with me if you want to live!" Tony shouts, throwing open the passenger door.

I leap for the open door...

And I'm lying there on top of my mattress, my dead laptop still open next to me on the bed. I'm dressed in yesterday's clothes, down to the Giants jersey.

And my phone is ringing. "Time to Run Amok." Tony's ringtone.

"Hey," I yawn into the phone. "What time is it?"

"Late enough that I've already been to church with Sabrina's family. And I owe her for skipping out on lunch, so you better come open the front door already."

Our doorbell rings out its five-note sequence from *Rites of Spring*.

I stumble to my feet and out the door of my room, but I can both feel and hear a discussion coming from the front door already. My mom and Tony.

Hoo boy.

That jolt of adrenaline wakes me up. I never got to tell Tony about that talk last night.

I slide down the bannister and make a hard left into the kitchen, where Tony already has a glass of orange juice. He's in jeans and a tee shirt that reads, "Former Sniper" on the front and "That's short for snipe hunter, right?" on the back.

Mom looks positively casual for a Sunday lunchtime. A beige Christian Dior dress instead of something like Versace, under her apron.

They both take one look at me and shake their heads. Mom points back upstairs.

"A shower. Go. Lunch will be here when you come down."

"Change of clothes wouldn't hurt either," says Tony.

I grumble my way back up to my room. In fact, I grumble through the quick shower too. I have to admit, though, that by the time I've got on sandals, a pair of blue plaid shorts, and a Three Coyotes tee shirt — from the tour in support of their third album, *Mete Locker*; the image includes a walk-in freezer full of medieval weapons — I do feel a bit better.

I've even worked out some of the muscle stiffness from a night on top of the mattress, fully dressed.

But when I come into the kitchen, there's a third person waiting for me. A man in a black suit and tie. He's got that ambiguous white male look — tall but not imposing, solid but not big, hair cropped short but not buzzed, clean shaven, enough chin to suggest strength, but not enough to remark on.

His eyes have taken my measure in the space of a single step. His thoughts are controlled. Smooth. Orderly.

He's the kind of man who could kill without changing his heartrate in the least.

"And this is my son," says Mom, in the tones she uses to introduce me to dignitaries.

"Good afternoon, Mr. Blackhall," he says, his tone as even and measured as his thoughts. "I'm Agent Johnson, but if you must ever refer to me in public, please refer to me as *Mister* Johnson. It could make the difference between life and death."

Something in the way he says that, the flow of his thoughts as he speaks sends a wave of cold across my face. I want to ask whose life and death, but I also don't want to ask. Because I get the feeling that he could mean innocent bystanders as easily as he could mean my life, or his.

"Good to meet you, Mr. Johnson."

"Please." He smiles, and for a moment he looks normal. Human. But the flow of his thoughts registers none of the usual changes people feel when they smile. "Don't let me stop you from eating your lunch. Your life needs to continue as normally as possible. I just need to ask you a few questions, and answer any of yours about how this is going to work."

"How what is going to work?"

I take my seat at the table, and Mom has arranged a good breakfast. Scrambled eggs with peppers, apple slices, and three kinds of cheese. Fresh squeezed orange juice, thick sliced bacon, and fresh baked sourdough bread. (Not baked by my mom, though. She hasn't baked since a spate of holiday fever a few years back.)

Tony has clearly finished his second plate. He both looks and feels concerned. I haven't seen Tony this concerned since he brought me home from the hospital after that coma last year.

"Now, officially," begins Agent Johnson, "you are not under anyone's investigation or protection. So it doesn't matter what agency I'm from, all right? This is off the books.

"I'm here with a team because your mother and father are very well connected, and when someone makes a death threat against their son, well, their highly placed friends take that seriously."

"Then why's it off the books," says Tony.

"Oh, it may become official later." Even this man's posture is unobtrusive. Straight, but not military straight. "Once we know what's going on. But the truth is, son, this may not be about you. This may be about your parents."

"Then why would my friends be dying?"

I swear, this guy is five seconds from me going into his head and finding out everything I want to know.

I'd do it right now, except that it just feels like a colossally bad move.

"Well, that's what we need to find out. Tell me about this club. There's nothing on the school records about you belonging to any clubs."

"Officially, I don't." I take a bite of bacon and decide to give this man something as close to the truth as I could manage. "Truth is, we heard about Skull and Keys, and wondered how that sort of thing gets started. So we would meet to discuss secret societies and our research about them. Thought it might be fun to try to start one."

"Did you?"

"Hardly. We never even got a full semester of research done because of classes. We'd just started to like hanging out together. It was more a laugh than anything else."

"What organizations did you research? What kind of research did you do?"

"Just library stuff. And online." Crap. What so-called secret societies can I think of? "The Masons, the Rosicrucians, Skull and Bones, Skull and Keys, the Oddfellows. I think that was all we really had. Took more than enough time to research even those groups."

Agent "Johnson" didn't write any of that down, but I had the feeling he didn't need to.

"How did you guys get along? Any couples in the group?"

"We got along all right, but not enough for dating."

"Mary Sugden was an attractive woman. You never asked her out?"

"I had a girlfriend."

"Name?"

"Amaris Silver."

"And she wasn't interested in your group?"

"She's a double-major. The only extra-curricular she had time for was me."

...and I just said that in front of my mother. I squeeze my eyes shut at the small noise of disapproval she makes and try to busy myself with my food.

"You refer to her in the past tense," says Agent Johnson, undeterred.

"We broke up," I say with my mouth full of scrambled eggs, then swallow. "It just didn't work out."

Because I'm a telepath and she's paranoid. Albeit with some reason, but not from me.

"Does your group have any enemies?"

"No one knew we existed."

"Past tense?"

"Half of us are dead, and Terrence has fled the country trying to save his own life."

"That was fast."

Fuck fuck fuck. Why did I have to mention Terrence?

"He didn't do it. During the school year he even volunteers at the Oakland police department."

"Your confidence in him is noted."

And I pick up from the agent's thoughts that he doesn't currently consider Terrence a suspect. But he'll note the information anyway, in case the investigation turns up something interesting.

"So how will ... this work?"

"Until this is resolved, anywhere you go there will be agents watching you. Do not look for them. You will not see them."

"He's very observant," says my mother. "Rick, tell Agent Johnson something he wouldn't expect you to notice."

I make a show of looking at him, while Agent Johnson looks back at me like a stone wall. But the answers are right there in his controlled, orderly thoughts.

"The slight bulge to your sock is not your backup piece. It's a distraction for professionals who would look for it there. All you have in your sock is a digital recorder, which is not currently running. Your backup piece is at the small of your back, hidden by the cut of your jacket."

A blink cracks Agent Johnson's stony façade.

"All right, I'm impressed. Eight out of ten of our own field agents wouldn't have gotten all of that. If you ever want to help stop the bad guys, Mr. Blackhall, have your parents tell their friends."

"I really think Sociology suits me better."

The last thing I want to do is spend my days around minds like yours, pal.

"Noted. But the offer will stand if you change your mind. For now, do not call attention to our agents if you notice them. Meanwhile we will have another team working the investigation to try to put this killer away as soon as possible.

"And for now, just go about your life as normal. Do what you would normally do on a day like this."

"Let's shoot some pool," says Tony.

I nod, drain my orange juice, and join him in heading for the game room.

But all the while I wonder if I should tell Agent Johnson about Hyun-Ki Noh.

BUT HYUN-KI NOH ISN'T THE ONLY ONE I HAVE TO WORRY ABOUT.

Agent Johnson. Or should I say Mister Johnson? Or should I say Agent "Johnson?"

I don't want to go into this guy's head. He's killed. I don't even have to find the dates, places and targets to know that. There's just something all through his aspect. Something I've never run across before.

Or maybe I have. Maybe Isla's "driver" has killed before. I could believe that of him.

But there's something different about this agent. Something colder. More distant. Maybe it's quantity, maybe it's motivation.

Or maybe there's just something different in this guy's psyche. Something I've never encountered before.

But I need to know what it is. I need to understand. Because this guy might be the only person between me and a killer with a high powered rifle.

And in some ways Agent Johnson *is* a high powered rifle. He feels like a loaded weapon, and I need to understand when and why he's likely to pull his trigger.

Fortunately I've already touched his mind, so I don't have to be near him to get back in. There's no way I could mistake that tight, controlled fog of thoughts for anyone else.

In fact, that his thoughts are so tight and controlled is worrying on its own. I'm used to that from telepaths. But this man is not a telepath.

So why are his thoughts like that?

I ponder going into Agent Johnson's head until Tony and I are down the hall, around the corner, and finally in the game room. Then I raise one hand so Tony knows to hold his questions.

And I reach for the mind of so-called Agent Johnson.

...damn near indefensible. He's in the backyard with my dad. Standing on the patio. Looking over the layout. *Eight shooting angles from rooftops we can't secure without raising questions from people who won't have to do their own asking. We should sneak that kid to a secure facility until the shooter's down.*

All right, so he's taking this seriously. And his name is actually Special Agent Colin McIntosh. "Johnson" is a code name for an NSA agent working in the field in an unofficial capacity.

NSA? This guy's from the freaking NSA?

Wait. I don't need to follow the NSA thread deeper into "Johnson's" mind. I don't need to get sidetracked.

But I do need to follow the thread about me. I need to know what he knows. What he suspects.

I don't have to go much deeper to get to his personal image profile of me. Long hair and love beads, with a protest sign in one hand and a trust fund checkbook in the other. A spoiled kid, talking about equality during the day and sleeping in four-star hotels at night. But there's a flag pin on the tie-dyed tee shirt. A pin that says I'm special. Important.

Agent Johnson might want to protect all American citizens, but I'm in the category he gives higher priority.

But no sign of telepathy...

Do I dare look?

Times like this, I wish the human mind came with a search engine. I can't just think of a word like telepathy and dig up results from his associations.

Well, actually I *could*. I could insert the word "telepathy" and see how he reacts, then follow the thread from there. But then he would be thinking about telepathy, which is the last thing I want. Especially if the word has any real meaning for him outside of movies like *Scanners* or *The Shining*.

So I can't work that directly or cleanly. I can't just pick a subject and see what there is to find. The human psyche is a mess of connections and connotations. Everything has meaning, and that meaning connects to other meanings.

I could find out why he thinks of me the way he does. The long hair. The love beads. Either of these will lead me to associations deeper in his mind. Clue me in about why he thinks this way and what it means.

But that won't get me to telepathy.

For that, I need a hook deeper into his mind. Something I can follow without just blindly charging ahead.

And the best place to start is with his self-image, not his thoughts of me.

Wait. No. It isn't. If I let myself get sidetracked with his life and personality, I'll be here all day. Or, at least what will feel like all day. I'll wear myself out, mentally, and it won't be twelve-thirty on a Sunday afternoon.

There's a better way.

Colin McIntosh, aka Agent Johnson, aka Mister Johnson, is a part of the NSA. That means ... ah, there it is. Tied into his team and the secondary team under his command for this unofficial mission.

Johnson's opinion of the NSA.

Pride hits me first. National pride, that feels uplifting. The kind of pride mixed with protective love, because his feelings about the NSA are tied into his feelings about the United States of America.

He was a marine sniper with Force Recon. He...

Wrong direction. I don't need to experience pulling the trigger in Afghanistan.

I backtrack into the NSA, away from the path that led him there. Instead I dig into the associations.

Pride. Protection. Investigation. Enemies foreign and domestic. Rules, and when to follow them...

Rules. Structure. Chain of command. Org chart. NSA. Governmental program.

YES! That's the key I've been looking for. The link from the NSA into Agent Johnson's greater sense of the NSA as a government program.

From there I can find other government programs. I riffle past the Internal Revenue Service, Federal Bureau of Investigation, Secret Service, Drug Enforcement Agency, Department of Homeland Security, Bureau of Alcohol, Tobacco and Firearms, Central Intelligence Agency...

Bingo. Follow that one.

Central Intelligence Agency. Conflict and sharing policies. Black projects...

MK Ultra.

Hypnosis. Mind control. Drugs. From what this guy knows about it, there was no attempt to develop telepathy here. It was all intelligence gathering work, based on controlling the mind in the kind of gross, ax-handle ways available to those without telepathic resources.

This isn't what I'm looking for.

I backtrack to the government agencies again. There was something else I need to find. Something involving "Jedi warriors" and a movie from a few years back.

Central Intelligence Agency, Defense Intelligence Agency…

Wait. Maybe that one.

There it is. The Stargate Project. I remember running across that on the web last year when I was desperately scrambling for any real information about telepathy. Before I realized that telepaths have no reason or motivation to post about telepathy on the internet. We can just talk to each other about it directly.

But what does Agent Johnson know about The Stargate Project?

A small red house in the Virginia suburb of Alexandria. On Oak Street, near a cul-de-sac. No one lives there. Two scientists show up every weekday morning at six a.m. One comes in by train. The other picks her up at the station and drives them both in. Red Buick, a few years out of date.

A minivan arrives every weekday at eight a.m. Driven by an agent. Six passengers. Four men. Two women.

Remote viewers, working for the military.

Agent Johnson has been that driver. On loan. Agent Johnson has been there as a perimeter guard too. Watching the neighborhood. Making sure it stays quiet and normal.

Johnson doesn't believe in remote viewing. Doesn't believe one person can sit in a recliner and watch submarine movements thousands of miles away. Read tomorrow's headlines. Contact another remote viewer in Los Angeles.

Hello. That's not some defunct project that no one has touched in forty years or more. That's a currently running program, funded somewhere within the vast budget of the federal government of the United States of America.

And that long distance contact? That's not remote viewing. That's telepathy.

But Johnson doesn't think of it that way. He sees it all as "that remote viewing crap."

I pull back from Johnson's mind.

My mom always wanted the game room to be as elegant as the

rest of the house. She put in the same high-end wooden flooring, plus soft brown paint with subtle red trim.

A pointless exercise. This room could never have maintained the elegance she strives for.

The game room has to accommodate all the children brought by party guests, sometimes as many as fifty kids of various ages and upbringings. So while the wainscoting and edging look great, the hard wood floor shows the scuff marks of countless games of tag and duck duck goose, random dancing and occasional fights.

Get past the forced manners of a diplomat's scion and you find a kid like any other.

Plus, although the tournament-size pool table does help give the room some class, it has to fight against the projection television with its four game consoles, the two pinball machines, the designated drawing/painting zone, and the air hockey table.

I've always thought the room was a bit schizophrenic.

Still, it's good to be here, and in my own head, instead of Agent Johnson's. He had way too many memory links that felt like they led places I didn't want to go.

Tony didn't get far during my quick check. In the brief moment I was in Agent Johnson's mind, Tony started toward the pool table to rack the balls for nine-ball.

—*We need to assume the room is bugged.*—

My voice in Tony's head makes him stiffen, but he continues toward the table and responds, *I will never get used to that.* A shudder moves through his shoulders. *All right though. We'll only talk about... Wait, they have to expect us to talk about what's going on.*

—*Yes, but don't mention telepathy. He doesn't know anything about it.*—

Tony nods and racks the balls.

"So where did Terrence run off to?"

"He wouldn't tell me." I toss Tony the quality guest cue and slip mine out of its case. "Just that with an assassin on his tail, sticking around seemed like the stupid move."

"He may have a point."

"Oh, please. Johnson practically has 'experienced professional' stamped on his forehead. What makes you think I could do better on my own?"

"Fine." Tony breaks without our usual lag to see who gets the first shot. He makes two, but ends up without a shot.

"Serves you right for not lagging."

I try to relax into the game while telepathically catching Tony up on some of what I've learned about "Agent Johnson."

Tony agrees that the appearance of a new telepath just as the murders start feels more than a little suspicious, but neither of us think that's enough to risk outing him to Agent Johnson.

I need more information, but how do I get it with federal agents — freaking NSA agents — dogging my every move? What if I make contact with Hyun-Ki and it turns out he *is* guilty? What if he takes the opportunity of contact to attack?

It would be awfully risky to have something bad happen — especially something bad and telepathic — while I'm under surveillance.

Mom and Dad meant well in calling in the big guns. And those big guns might just save my life, it's true.

So why do I feel like they're chains around my ankles?

I puzzle over that while Tony and I play. After I beat him seven games out of nine at nine-ball, we switch to a one hundred point game of fourteen-one, continuous. One of the most demanding games in pool, it requires focus, skill, planning, and the ability to get out of terrible situations.

In other words, it's a great distraction from serious thoughts.

By the halfway mark of the game, I'm actually starting to feel that I might be able to figure all this out. With guards keeping an eye on my physical body, maybe I just need to start sending my thoughts out to see what I can find? Follow one mind to another until it leads me somewhere solid.

If I can find the killer's mind, I can end all this without anyone else getting hurt.

I'm just about to tell Tony that when Agent Johnson bursts through the door.

"Mr. Blackhall, do you know a Darcy Sullivan of 3223 Zelazny Drive in the Berkeley Hills?"

My stomach drops straight through the floor. My face goes cold. My lips barely move when I answer.

"I don't know that address. But I do know Darcy."

"Then I'm afraid your friend was just shot dead. Two bullets from a high powered rifle. Heart and head.

"And we need to talk."

8

———————

"What the hell aren't you telling me?"

I'm sitting in the kitchen again, and from the smell, someone's been using the orange cleaner. That's unusual. Mom usually lets me clean up my own breakfast, even if I leave the dishes out for a while.

Tony has to wait in the game room. He's pacing. Scared. Mom is off doing something in the back of the house, and I can feel Dad in the garage, trying to keep busy.

Dad knows something's up, but Mom doesn't. That's unusual.

The only physical sign that Agent Johnson is angry with me is that he has his hands on his hips. His face is smooth. His tone is steady. I doubt his pulse is higher than sixty right now.

Of course, his thoughts are whirling. Restrained anger. He thinks I'm treating this as some kind of game.

Me, my pulse is going a mile a minute, and my body feels like it's trying to fall into my grave and leave me standing here without it.

First Mary. Then Jamal. Now Darcy.

Why?

"You're holding something back from me, Mr. Blackhall. I need to know what it is. Now."

"I really don't know what you mean."

Crap, he can tell I'm lying. His thoughts are focusing harder on my face. Studying.

"Look." He lets out a deep sigh, and his tone shifts to commiserating. Sympathetic.

Of course, his thoughts stay wary and focused. This is all an act.

"You're scared. And you have reason to be." He pulls out a chair, spins it around, and sits on it so his arms are resting on the chair back. "This killer is good. A pro. Someone wants you and your friends dead. And right now it looks like that is *going* to happen."

He reached out and gives my shoulder a shake.

"I can help you. I can protect you. But I have to have all the information. Otherwise ... otherwise it's like I'm playing a race to nine with the killer and I've spotted him seven games."

Wow. A pool reference. I didn't expect that.

"I don't know." I really let my frustration and fear out in that one sentence. But then I inhale as deeply as I can and let the breath out slowly.

"Maybe I know more than I think I do. But how am I supposed to know what's important and what isn't? I mean, last year I roomed with a shooting guard on Cal's basketball team, and both Jamal and I played pick-up games with them on off-days. Maybe that's related? Maybe Mary and Darcy dated players and I didn't know that?"

"You let me worry about the connections." He feels confident now. Assured that I'm ready to help. "Now, how did you know Darcy? You didn't mention her as part of your club."

Oh, God. Darcy's dead.

All my telepath friends are dying.

I'm crying again, and I hate myself for it. Shame burns through me at the thought of bawling here like a baby in front of a federal agent, but the shame isn't enough to stop my chest from heaving with the sobs.

Agent Johnson hands me a handkerchief. Pats me on the shoulder.

"I'm sorry," he says. "I don't like having to do this to you. I don't like telling you that your friend is dead, and I especially don't like having to interrogate you about it. If I had my way, I'd be out there chasing your killer and keeping you safe.

"That's why I do what I do. So good people like you don't have to see their friends get killed." He squeezes my shoulder. "But I *need* your help to keep you safe. So I'm going to have to ask you these questions anyway. And you're going to have to do your best to answer them. Now how did you know Darcy?"

"There were a few more of us, winter semester. We didn't think of ourselves as a club then, and we weren't trying to form anything. Just a few people with similar interests. As soon as we started getting serious, the others dropped out."

"Darcy was one of these others?" When I nod, he says, "Who were the others?"

"Kelly Hammond and Stephen DeFaustino. I kept in touch with Darcy, but not those two."

"What did your girlfriend think of that?" At my blank look, he adds, "Darcy Sullivan was reportedly beautiful enough to get modeling gigs when she wanted them. Did your girlfriend object to you maintaining a friendship with someone so good-looking?"

"No. For the same reason Amaris didn't mind me hanging out with Candi Sayer. There was nothing romantic there."

I spot the place in Agent Johnson's fog of thoughts where he takes his notes. Fascinating.

"Who was your roommate? The basketball player."

"Karif Awad."

Agent Johnson not only notes that, I watch as his mind highlights it and try not to let my irritation with his profiling show.

And the moment I think of profiling, I feel guilty for even suspecting Hyun-Ki. Of course he wasn't involved. And if I had any doubts, he had no reason to have any idea who Darcy was. Not from the information I sent him about BTO.

"You got along well with Mr. Awad?"

"Still do. He's coming to stay with us for a couple of weeks before school starts. You can ask my parents about him. He's a good guy."

"People only show you the face they want you to see, Mr. Blackhall. Friends and enemies alike."

Agent Johnson exhales sharply and stands up.

"All right, Mr. Blackhall, you've given me some good leads to follow for now." He raises a warning finger. "But if you think of anything else. Anything at all, no matter how trivial. That you had in common with Mary, Jamal and Darcy, you need to tell me ASAP.

"It might mean the difference between life and death for you or one of your friends."

He leaves me thinking about that. And wondering.

If I had mentioned Darcy earlier, would she still be alive? Does he need to know how we're really connected? We all talk about not outing one another, but is keeping silent about telepathy worth all these lives?

Should I tell him about my telepathy?

Before I can even consider telling anyone else about my own knack, I should check with the only other telepaths I know.

So I don't even get up from the kitchen table when I reach out for Terrence's mind.

I find it, which alone is enough to help me sigh out some of my tension. Even before I "knock" I can feel that Terrence is at least as stressed out as I am.

He doesn't answer.

I try again, sending him the memory of me, knocking on Tony's door. It's sophomore year in high school, and I'm excited about a camping trip and have news for Tony.

What? The undercurrent is as terse as the word.

—I have news. Have a second?—

Only a second. Go.

—Darcy's dead. My parents have people here to protect me. You should come. They'll protect you too.—

People? What people? What aren't you telling me?

I'm getting that question a lot lately.

—They're government agents...—

Fuck you!

—But they aren't here officially.—

Don't let them snow you. Feds are always official. You better keep your mouth shut about telepathy and about me, or else. And you can fuck off now.

He cuts the contact. Wow. A threat from Terrence. Either he's more stressed out about this than I thought, or he's even more scared of becoming a government lab rat than I am.

So much for that then.

I'm about to reach for Hyun-Ki's mind when my phone starts playing "Dracula's Tango" by Zombina and the Skeletones.

Amaris' ringtone.

"Hey," I say as I answer.

"Why are MiBs asking me about you?"

I hadn't thought about that. Do NSA agents count as Men in Black?

"Because they're talking to just about everyone I know. Someone's trying to kill me."

"Tell them to get in line... Wait. You're serious, aren't you?"

"Unfortunately." I sigh and put my feet up on the chair Agent Johnson has vacated. "They've already gotten Jamal, Mary and Darcy."

Incomplete silence. I can hear vague voices in the background, but I can't tell where she is. Yet again, I wish telepathy over the phone were as easy and casual as it is in person. But from here I can't find out what she's up to without actual effort.

Effort Amaris would not appreciate.

"I'm sorry about the other two of your friends," she says at last. "But I hope Mary burns in hell."

"You're probably not the only one."

She scoffs. "You know, I could probably have forgiven your role in all this if you'd been as mad at her as I am. If you'd cut her off like the bitch she was. If you'd just taken my side—"

"I was always on your side. I was furious with her over what she did."

"Didn't feel like it. Not once I knew the truth about the night we met. Just felt like you were making excuses..."

Amaris blows out a deep breath.

"Look. I didn't call to fight with you, Rick. Are you in trouble? My mom and dad aren't without connections of their own."

Amaris' dad is a pretty big name televangelist. Her parents have a set of friends and connections that probably rivals my own parents'. Albeit very different people.

"I'm surprised you're offering. You made it clear that I'm *persona non grata*."

"That doesn't mean I want to see you dead. Jokes aside, we had some good times. And those were real, whatever the circumstances on the night we met."

"I never meant to hurt you. I'm sorry I didn't tell you sooner."

"Tell me what?"

Wait. The agents came to see Amaris. Amaris who was murderously angry at Mary when she learned that Mary used some telepathic suggestion to send her to a certain party on a certain night, open to the possibility of a one-night stand. A party where Mary knew I would be, and Mary knew that Amaris had seen me and thought I was hot.

Amaris would probably have gone on at length about telepathy and telepaths to those federal agents, except for one thing.

I won't let her.

Allowing Amaris her righteous anger at Mary — and arguably at me — is one thing. Letting her blab to anyone and everyone that Mary and I are telepaths? And that there are others?

That was a risk I couldn't take.

So I left a few subtle blocks in place that kept her from communicating anything at all about telepathy to anyone but me, and only then in complete and total assured privacy, if I brought the subject up.

But Amaris is smart. Smart enough to know that if federal agents are watching me, my phone is probably tapped.

Smart enough to try to lure me into tipping the truth.

"How sorry I am about what Mary did to you. How I should have told you sooner. How even though I meant everything I ever said to you, that one omission was a sin for which I can never repent enough.

"I did love you, Amaris. For whatever that's worth."

She hangs up on me.

I stare at my phone for a moment. Wondering if she was counting on the phone tap. Wondering if the agents are next to her right now. Wondering how she would try to get around the block next time.

Wondering if my biggest mistake was not telling her sooner? Or not erasing all the evidence when the whole thing blew up?

Either way, I better go catch Tony and my parents up or someone's going to have an aneurysm.

9

———

I'm scared to leave my own home.

It's almost midnight right now, and for the first time in months, I haven't left my house on a Sunday.

Tony's gone home. Or over to Sabrina's, maybe. Agent Johnson doesn't consider him a likely target. My best friend, but not a Berkeley connection. No tie to my "club."

My parents have asked about a zillion questions. Agent Johnson has added even more to the mix.

I can't keep it all straight anymore. I've been crying and shaking in turns. My guts feel like they've been shredded.

I want to contact Jamal's brother Jice, but I've never met him. Can't think of what I'd say to him if I could think of a way to get in touch.

I'm sorry your brother's dead? You were right not to join the BTO, because someone is killing us off, one by one?

I'm exhausted, but I can't sleep. I'm stretched thin. Like someone ran me through a pasta maker twice, then tugged around the edges all evening to get as much surface area out of the dough as possible. So thin you could see through me if you held me up to the light.

I didn't even eat much dinner. Or any. I think I had a peanut butter sandwich in there sometime, because I can still taste a bit of peanut stuck to a tooth.

I haven't felt this bad since I first developed telepathy and couldn't control it.

I wanted to die then.

I might die now.

At the moment I'm lying on top of my bedspread still in my Three Coyotes shirt and plaid blue shorts. The drapes are closed because they have to be. Agent Johnson ordered it. No open drapes anywhere in the house until the killer is down.

And as of right now, the killer is not down.

As of right now, the killer is running this show.

Agent Johnson won't admit it, but his people are at a loss. The killer must have been planning his hits for days. Maybe weeks. He knew when and where to find his targets. He left behind no evidence, not even a shell.

Well, except in the case of Mary's murder. Then he didn't just leave behind a shell casing. He left behind a whole pistol. Colt Desert Eagle. Forty-five caliber. They traced it to a gang of Hells Angels that operates out of Oakland. They claim the pistol was an inheritance, and stolen from them.

Dead end.

A witness too, but the witness never saw the actual killer. Only the "mugger." Who is now dead.

Another dead end.

Johnson figures the killer knows my parents would call in help. Must be figuring their work into his plans.

Johnson — or should I call him McIntosh? — won't say any of that out loud, of course. I started pulling facts from his head around eight o'clock.

I think it was eight o'clock.

Anyway, I got sick of the waiting and wanted to know what was going on.

The agent believes me now. Believes I'm scared enough to tell him anything. Has no idea how important it is to me to keep silent about telepathy.

Right or wrong, I'm not saying a fucking word about it.

Anyway, "Johnson's" men are doing the best they can with the information they have.

Which isn't enough.

But telling them I'm a telepath won't help. Won't get them what they need. It'll just put a target on my head. Get me swooped up in the night or something and deposited in Alexandria, Virginia, where I'll show up at a little red house every morning in a minivan, so I can tell some scientists what world leaders are thinking or where the troops are moving or what Al Qaeda is up to or some damn thing like that.

And that would be my life. Until they retire me the way the killer wants to. Bullet to the head. Protect state secrets.

"Top state secret. Confidential." Just like *The Prisoner.* The old one. With Patrick McGoohan. Retire me to some tiny island for people who know too much.

All right, when I'm comparing my life to Sixties television shows, I've sunk about as low as I'm going to allow. Just because there really is an active Project Stargate doesn't mean the government wants to kill me or "retire" me someday.

Not that I'm willing to take that chance.

And if I want to live long enough to decide one way or the other, I need to do something besides sit here and worry and mourn my dead friends.

They would expect more of me than that. Mary would expect me to exact holy vengeance on all involved with the perpetrators.

Jamal would at least expect me to take down the killer and the money man.

The money man.

That's it.

There has to be a money man. Agent Johnson keeps going on and on about how professional the killer is. I've been thinking about this in terms of who would want us dead. But just as important is the question of who could arrange it.

Pete and Repeat might want Mary dead, if they found out what she did to them. But while they might have arranged the fake mugging, they aren't likely to be able to arrange a professional hit man for the rest of us. Not on a campus cop's salary.

Kelly never had any money to speak of. He wasn't hurting or anything, but wasn't rolling in it either.

Certainly not enough for this kind of thing. And that's assuming he had any way of knowing how to arrange it.

But what about Stephen?

Stephen, the man who would have founded a whole telepathic race with himself as king. Stephen, who had no ethical qualms about enslaving a married couple to tend to his every need.

Stephen, whom I put into a coma after I ripped the telepathy right out of his head.

I drag my feet over the side of the bed and drop them on the floor, tightening my gut enough that the process makes me sit up.

Stephen *would* do this. Stephen might even have the money to do this. But would Stephen have the knowhow?

It's not like he could hire a murderer off of Drewslist.

Well, maybe he could. But that killer would more likely be a beat-them-to-death-with-a-baseball-bat kind of thug than a big league hitman who can baffle freaking NSA agents.

The point is, it takes a certain kind of connection to hire that sort of killer.

And there's only one way to find out if Stephen has those connections.

I reach out to Stephen's mind.

No defenses at all. That's so weird. I haven't been into Stephen's head since the day of our big fight. He was a damned good telepath then — however much we would never see eye-to-eye about the rights and wrongs of our powers, I had to admit that the boy had skills.

And now I slip right up to his fog of thoughts and I can tell he doesn't even know I'm here.

He's in bed, but not yet asleep. He's reading *Influence* by Michael Shea. He's not alone either. There's someone next to him. A girl. She's... Tina.

I remember Tina. She was Kelly's "practice project," a generously proportioned young Latina woman of ... easy virtue.

Guess she traded up from Kelly, once telepathy was out of the equation.

I'm tempted to see what I can learn by slipping into Tina's mind first, but the poor girl has suffered enough already.

So I go into Stephen's mind.

His surface thoughts are all full of ideas about manipulation, his own extrapolations from the things he's been reading.

Rick, I presume that's you.

Wait, he *can* tell I'm here? But he doesn't feel like a telepath.

I've been waiting for this contact, and believe me, I remember very well what it felt like to have another person's mind touch mine. But as you know I have no more access to the talents that God gave me, so if it is you Rick, you'll just have to tell me.

I assume this has something to do with those two federal agents who came by the house today...

—Hello, Stephen.—

Ah, good. I thought that was you. I did so hope it was. This conversation would have meant so much less if Terrence had thought to contact me first.

—You said something about federal agents? What did they want with you?—

Laughter, much more nasal than when he used to have more control. Probably closer to his real laugh.

Come now, Rick. They came to find out what I know and determine whether or not I'm a suspect. They think I am, of course. The rejected applicant to your little club, or whatever fiction you've spun for them.

And there it is. The truth hiding just behind his thoughts, where once he might have been able to hide it.

—*So it is you. You're the one behind the assassin.*—

Who else? Kelly? Your dear Amaris?

—*You'll fry for this.*—

Not likely. You have no proof, and you'll never get any. I'm not a fool, you know. While the rest of you were off playing games about right and wrong, I was setting up contingencies. Such as money. Did Jamal ever tell you I'd arranged an annual income for myself well into the seven figures?

No? I'm not surprised. He probably saw it as harmless enough. A severance package for me after you tore my superior talent to shreds with a lucky maneuver.

Anger now. Hot anger. But burning coffee hot, not white phosphorous hot like a proper telepath would have been able to project.

And that wasn't all. The gift allowed me to walk into all the most dangerous places in perfect safety. To meet with the most dangerous men and get them to trust me. And assure myself of their loyalty.

So dig through my skull all you want, fool. You won't find any direct connection to the assassin. I have no way of canceling the contract even if I wanted to, and the money is off somewhere in an escrow account under someone else's name. I don't even know if your killer will be a man or a woman.

But I can tell you this much. I have no phone in the house. Even Tina isn't allowed to bring one when she comes over. And I am under surveillance by my own "private security."

And if my surveillance team catches even a hint of me doing anything out of the ordinary. If I so much as leave the house to get my newspaper. If anything like that happens, Rick Blackhall, anything that could possibly help you survive this — I'll be dead before I accomplish it.

And it will just look like the assassin got me too.

You are going to die for what you did to me, Rick. You and every other telepath I can find.

If I can't have this power, no one can.

I don't bother replying to Stephen's monologue. The key to stopping this assassin is somewhere in his head. It must be.

I just have to find it.

One thing, at least, is on my side right now. Stephen is not only pleased and proud of his assassin, but he believes I can't find anything in his head to help me stop his killer.

So he's not doing anything to hide...

Wait.

That doesn't sound like Stephen at all.

He knows I have the advantage here. He knows I can dig through his mind and find every tiny fact that might make a difference. Even the seemingly small and innocuous bits that he might not realize are there.

He knows all this.

He also knows I can only spend so much time digging through his head. Even the dream speed of a deep probe can only help so much when his mind contains volumes of data that would fill every computer storage device on earth to capacity and beyond.

So there's no way he's going to help me out by pointing me right to the connections that I need to follow to get what I need.

He's going to distract me all he can. Send me down every wrong avenue and path he can trick me into focusing on.

But at the same time, he needs his false leads to come close enough to the real information to ring true. Anything blatantly useless will stand out too much.

So once more Stephen is using half-truths to make his point.

I just need to figure out which is which.

All right. I know that any attempt to control Stephen and make him try to call off the contract will end in his death. I can feel the blunt truth of that in his head. It tastes like cough medicine. Syrupy.

He really does have a surveillance team ready to kill him. Or at least he believes he does.

Wish I could just slip into *their* heads. If I could stop them I could make Stephen turn himself in. Let the professionals figure out the rest.

But he doesn't know who the team is. He's never contacted their minds, and they aren't physically close enough to him for me to detect.

I wonder if I could send someone over to Stephen's house? Someone with a cell phone, that I could then make Stephen use to call the police and turn himself in...

That's a risk. If anything went wrong, I could be murdering a stranger for a *chance* at turning Stephen in.

I'm not willing to risk that stranger's life.

So what else do I know?

The assassin is paid for, and Stephen doesn't know the killer's identity. That much is certain too.

But the rest. His feelings about the rest aren't quite so clear. A bunch of emotions underneath the points he wanted to make.

I slip back through the main content of his little monologue.

While the rest of you were off playing games about right and wrong, I was setting up contingencies. Such as money.

He wants me to believe the assassin is a contingency plan. Like his income. He wants me to focus on the income. On wondering what other contingencies he's set up...

There's something in there he doesn't want me to notice.

What else did he say?

The gift allowed me to walk into all the most dangerous places in perfect safety. To meet with the most dangerous men and get them to trust me. And assure myself of their loyalty.

So dig through my skull all you want, fool. You won't find any direct connection to the assassin. I have no way of canceling the contract even if I wanted to, and the money is off somewhere in an escrow account under someone else's name. I don't even know if your killer will be a man or a woman.

Of course. It's so simple.

Stephen is presenting these facts the way he wants me to interpret them. He speaks as though he personally walked into those seedy bars and massage parlors and businesses that were little more than fronts for criminal activity, trusting to his powers to keep him safe.

But that would have been foolish. It would have given these dangerous people a face and a name to connect with him. It would have expanded the margins of error in his plans.

And it would have introduced the risk of a physical attack he lacked the time to prepare for.

He had no reason to risk all that. Especially since he could walk into these places in someone else's head. Let someone else be the puppet, speaking directly to the people involved while Stephen sat in safety.

Then even a surprise knife in the back would not have amounted to anything worse than an inconvenience.

Only one problem I see with that scenario.

Once Stephen lost his powers, he would also have lost his ability to control his patsy.

Unless the patsy were someone known to him. Someone deferential. Someone who would bow to Stephen's stronger personality even once Stephen lacked the power to back up his control.

Someone like Kelly.

WELL, IT'S NOT KELLY.

I probably should have known that. After all, why risk any telepath at all — even one as weak as Kelly was — when the "normals" abound, just waiting for a superior mind to slip in and take over.

I swear, Stephen actually thinks this way. The fact that he's no longer a telepath hasn't done anything to restrain his ego.

But I had to check. And I wasted a good half-hour of real time sifting through Kelly's memories and hopes and plans as I tried to determine if he has any connection at all to the assassinations taking place among his former friends.

Kelly does know what's going on. What he doesn't know is how Stephen is pulling it off. But he's impressed as hell by it all the same.

In fact, he has such a bad case of hero-worship going for Stephen that he thinks Stephen deserved to "steal" Tina from him.

These two are so dysfunctional I can barely handle contact with their minds.

And the fact is, I'm exhausted. Way too tired to be pushing myself the way I am.

I mean, first there's the emotional roller coaster I've been on for the last couple of days. Then add to that my lack of sleep, and my lack of proper nutrition while I've been unable to eat anything more than a nibble.

Now factor in the telepathic effort of all this deep digging. And I've already done so much of it I feel as though I've spent days or weeks sifting through Kelly's memories alone.

All I want to do is sleep. Just close my eyes and make the world go away for a few days. Maybe a week. Hide here in my bedroom while the professionals take care of my problem for me.

But I can't do that.

Because I saw something else in Stephen's mind while I was in there. Backup targets. Amaris. Tony. Jenna. My parents. If I'm unavailable as a target for too long, the assassin will start killing people I care about.

I can't let that happen.

I just wish I could end this without any more contact with minds as foul as Stephen and Kelly. I want to get myself clear of their crap once and for all. I just want to pull back into my own mind for a while and try to remember what clean feels like.

But that's not a luxury I can afford.

Because if Kelly isn't my answer, I have to go back into Stephen's head and figure out what is.

I really don't want to do that. I just don't see any viable alternatives.

So back into Stephen's memories I go, looking for any clues I can find that will help lead me to a killer.

STEPHEN STARTED WITH BRIEF PHYSICAL VISITS TO POLICE DEPARTMENTS, first in Berkeley, then in Oakland, Richmond, and Emeryville.

In each case he used a false name to report a stolen bicycle, then wiped the memory of the incident from the officer he spoke to and buried the paperwork.

In this way, he gave himself an in with the local police departments in a way they would not later connect with him.

Then he began head-hopping his way through the police departments to find gang information. Not looking for the street stuff. The drug stuff. The prostitution. No, he wanted to find the RICO suspects. Anyone connected high enough to have the police hoping to pin a racketeering charge was likely to have the connections needed to accomplish whatever underworld activities Stephen might find useful.

But he didn't want those people. He wanted to know where they were found. He figured if he could do that, he could find the real players. The ones the cops can't even finger yet.

That took a while. But ultimately he found a garage in Oakland on 17th that served as an important meeting spot.

From there Stephen infiltrated the head of Larry "Goldtooth" Whitman. A fixer, with a big smile and a gold front tooth. Goldtooth never gets his hands dirty himself, but he "knows a guy who knows a guy" who can get just about anything done.

Middle management in his criminal organization. Perfect for Stephen's purposes.

Stephen spent weeks working on Goldtooth. Laying and layering controls deep in Goldtooth's subconscious. He treated it like programming, complete with variables.

At this point, Stephen could send Goldtooth a coded message through an "anonymous" phone call, a paper message, a radio "request" song, any one of a number of ways. Goldtooth would destroy any evidence without thinking about it.

And Stephen has four other guys like Goldtooth in the East Bay.

But in this case, the most important element of Goldtooth's programming is a key phrase: "Faust beckons you." Anyone who says that phrase to Goldtooth gets treated with the deferential obedience that Stephen considers his due.

Stephen also has a set of delivery men conditioned to obey him in all things. Delivery men who can walk into or out of almost anywhere unquestioned.

In this case, a delivery man named Hector Maldonado was the key player. It all went down like this:

Stephen had money transferred to an offshore account listed by a number, not a name. One million dollars per target.

He gave the number and the target list to Kelly. Kelly gave them to Hector Maldonado, along with a trigger phrase that means nothing on its own: "This week's fantasy football roster. Pure gold."

"Pure gold" meant to deal with Goldtooth. "Football roster" meant that these were people who had to die, and in this order. "Fantasy" meant that only the best would do for the job.

Goldtooth handled the rest. He would never remember setting it up. Neither would Maldonado. That was part of the programming, to provide another layer of protection between Stephen and any criminal activities he commissioned. Anything that came in through his codes vanished from conscious memory after being completed.

Only another telepath could dig it out. If that telepath knew where to look.

And Stephen set this all up ahead of time, just in case he ever needed it.

If I felt any qualms about having taken away this man's powers, they're gone now.

He wasn't kidding. I don't think I can tie this to him.

Kelly didn't do anything that could be considered illegal. Neither did Maldonado. Goldtooth did, but doesn't remember what, much less whom he hired to do the job.

Stephen's mind is a dead end. He insulated himself too well.

If I could get to that garage in Oakland, I could meet Goldtooth. Then I could actually get into his head and try to accomplish something.

But how would I explain it to kindly Agent Johnson and the NSA?

Pardon me, guys, I just need to take a road trip to a garage in Oakland to meet someone involved with organized crime. No, I don't need to talk to him. I just need to get close to him for a moment. I don't even have to actually see him, though life would be easier if I did.

Yes, this has to do with the person trying to kill me. But I can't tell you how or why.

What's that? If I know that and I don't tell you everything, then I'm guilty of aiding and abetting?

Yeah. This just sounds like a great idea to me.

I can't even give them Goldtooth's name, because I couldn't explain how I'd gotten it or why I didn't give it to them sooner.

—*I have to hand it to you, Stephen. You isolated yourself well from this.*—

I could still call it off, you know. He feels smug, self-satisfied as a bloated tick. *If you give me back my powers I just might.*

—*I could do that. I never told Jamal, but I figured out how to repair the damage. In fact, I could probably give telepathy to someone who was born without it.*—

Excitement burbles though Stephen. Childish glee.

Perfect. Just do that then and I'll call the hit off. Then you and I can work together. There's so much I could teach you, Rick.

I can feel the lie underneath his words. He wants revenge, however much he's trying to hide it.

Or we could go our separate ways. The world is more than big enough to two alpha telepaths like us.

I send him echoing raucous laughter until he quiets down, seething in his rage.

—*Never. Not even if I believed you would really call off the hit. Even if I believed you could.*—

—*You killed them. Mary. Jamal. Darcy. Hell, maybe Terrence by now. Maybe your killer has been off fulfilling that part of the contract while I've been in hiding someplace you can never touch me.*—

—*No, Stephen*— I lied, —*I just wanted you to know I could* do *it, and*

I won't. And I won't send you out there to be killed by your contingency squad, so you can die pretending to still be a telepath.—

—I'm going to find a way to stop your killer. And I'm going to build the kind of telepathic community you could only dream of, free from bullshit like yours.—

—But you won't live to see it.—

—This is what you're going to do, you son of a bitch. First you're going to send Tina home. Then you're going to make out a quick will, leaving ten percent of your total wealth to Tina. Another ten percent to Summer Jones, to pay for your part in the crimes committed on her by Kelly.—

—You'll give another twenty percent to the couple you abused for housing, sex and whatever else.—

—And the rest you'll leave to the Cal Scholarship Fund.—

—You'll sign that will, scan it or snap a picture of it, and send it to your lawyer, swearing you are doing this of your own free will.—

—And then, you bastard, you are going to commit suicide. You are going to sit in the tub and slash your own jugular. You will continue to cut until your arm lacks strength to go on.—

I reinforce the commands, then sever the connection to his mind.

I stumble into my bathroom, throw open the toilet, and throw up bile until I don't have even that left in my stomach.

I'm shaky and sweaty and cold and so tired I can barely think straight.

I just committed murder.

But God help me, that man had to die.

10

———

I'm on the white tile floor of my bathroom, my head resting on the red rug in front of my toilet. Resting's a bad term for it though. I'm stiff and sore through my neck and shoulders and back. My skin's clammy, and rough with sweat salt.

And I'm still dressed in yesterday's clothes.

Or is it today's clothes?

The light's on. And the fan. But the skylight up above shows me a pale blue sky.

Daytime then.

I smell stale puke. And that I need a shower.

Why did I fall asleep here?

My phone rings, and I realize it woke me up.

The ringtone is "Who Am I?" by Three Coyotes. Not the house phone then. My phone, and an unknown caller.

I consider letting it ring.

Then it peals off again and I'm moving before I can think. My neck kinks harder, and I think I left my brain back there on the carpet — or maybe in the toilet — but I'm leaning on my dresser and my phone is in my hand, holding it up to my ear.

"Hello?" I croak.

"Rick?" The voice is familiar. A girl's. "This *is* Rick Blackhall's phone?"

"Ye—" I turn and cough to clear my throat. But my mouth is so dry I don't sound much better when I continue. "Yeah, this is me. Who is calling?"

"Sounds like *someone* had a rough night." I can hear the smile on her face. "This is Isla. We met Saturday?"

"Of course," I say, while my system tries to process yet one more shock, and fails. My whole body feels like it's on hold and will get back to me later. "What can I do for you, Isla?"

"It's what you already did. Turns out my security guy Hank *was* keeping an eye on my agent, but he couldn't put his finger on why until we started talking about it.

"Turns out my agent has been using hints of my possible involvement in projects to negotiate better terms for his other clients. *Without* my knowledge and consent."

"Holy crap."

"Yes, he's not my agent anymore, and I've spread the word in a few key circles."

"Wow."

The sharp pains in my neck and shoulders are stealing too much attention from the conversation. I can't think of anything to say, and I can't even begin to make headway into rubbing these muscles right now.

But Isla laughs.

"Let me guess. Not only did I wake you up, but you were up late."

"...something like that."

"I see." Her voice gets teasing. "Was there a girl involved?"

"I wish."

The moment the words are out of my mouth I try to bite my tongue to recall them. But that never works. I do thump my forehead, and immediately wish I hadn't. The pain reverberates all the way down my torso.

"Good. Then no one will accuse me of poaching if I want to take you out to a thank-you dinner."

"Dinner?"

"Yes," she says with a laugh. "Hank was weeks away from feeling sure enough of his suspicions to say anything, and your perceptivity may have saved my business reputation. I happen know the best Chinese restaurant in San Francisco, and I want to take you there Friday night. Sound good?"

"...yes."

"Excellent. I'll pick you up at seven. Dress sharp."

When she says goodbye the word has a teasing quality that suggests this dinner might be more than a business thank you.

When I hang up I stare at the phone. Not sure if that just happened or if this is some fever dream. That the time is nine-oh-five a.m. on a Monday morning doesn't tell me.

Then I catch another whiff of myself and know it isn't a dream. In my dreams I don't stink like puke and a day of hard labor.

Slowly, to avoid angering my various unhappy muscles any further, I strip out of yesterday's clothes and wander back toward the bathroom for a much needed shower.

I hope scalding hot water can make some headway into my many knotted muscles.

A half-hour shower and a fistful of ibuprofen later my body is still mad at me, but at least we're now on speaking terms. I almost feel human again, if more than a little strung out and hungry.

I'm dressed in a plain gray tee shirt and plain gray sweat shorts, making my way downstairs to the kitchen.

Agent Johnson is waiting for me, leaning against a cabinet.

His greeting is friendly enough, and he has the courtesy to wait until I've filled a bowl with a honey-nut bran cereal and sat down at the table before he hits me with more news.

"Stephen DeFaustino is dead."

I finish a sip of orange juice. I don't try to keep the fatigue out of my voice.

"Another assassination?"

"No, actually." His brow furrows down. "It seems that late last night he modified his will and sent it to his attorney. His attorney thought the changes seemed unusual, and paid him a visit this morning. The front door was unlocked. Mr. DeFaustino was dead in his bathroom. Suicide."

"Suicide?" I set my spoon back in the bowl, guilt gnawing somewhere low in my bowels. "Any idea why?"

"No note. And attorney-client privilege keeps the changes to the will secret until his estate is finalized."

"Oh."

"The will sounds guilty though. Gave away everything to his girlfriend, three other non-relations, and a scholarship fund."

"I thought you said—"

"Officially neither I nor anyone on my team has seen it. But officially I'm not even here." He tilts his head slightly. "When was the last time you spoke with Mr. DeFaustino?"

"Haven't seen him in months. Once he was out of the group, he was out of the group. We didn't exactly exchange numbers."

It's getting easier to lie with half-truths. I'm not sure that's a good thing.

"Someone did call you this morning though."

"Isla Perkins." I blink rapidly. "Why? Do you think she's involved?"

Agent Johnson looks at me, and though his straight face reveals nothing his thoughts clearly reflect one idea — he can barely comprehend the life I lead. A life where a pop star calls me to ask me for a date. Even though he could poll a thousand citizens and not find one who recognizes my name.

Of course, I could tell Agent Johnson that this is a unique occurrence. But then I would have to explain to him why I felt the need to share that detail with him.

"I consider her involvement unlikely," he says, though his tone suggests that pop stars committing assassination-style murders isn't something he considers out of the realm of possibility.

"But the timing is interesting. Of his suicide I mean. Most of the members of your group are dead, but not all of them. In fact, there's a lull in the killings, and suddenly he commits suicide. And leaves the bulk of his not-inconsiderable estate to charity."

"I wouldn't have expected Stephen to know any assassins."

Agent Johnson shakes his head.

"No one knows assassins. They know people who can hire some-one. And you can never tell who knows the right people. But believe me, by the end of the day my people will know everything there is to know about the late Stephen DeFaustino. If he was involved, we'll find out."

I choose not to express the extent of my doubts.

"I hope so." I close my eyes and let it all out in one sentence. "I would love to be out from under the sword of Damocles."

"What are your plans for the day?"

I make him wait through a spoonful of cereal.

"Free throws. Lots of free throws. Then, I don't know. Maybe a hike." I turn to look at him directly. "Would that be a bad idea?"

"Depends on the park. I'll help you figure out a route before you go."

I nod, and keep eating.

"Do my parents know about Stephen?"

"No. I suggested very strongly that they go back to work today. They consented to a half-day as long as I stick near you myself. They'll be back around one."

I go back to eating. I note he hasn't told me about any progress on the case. Just more questions.

My silence must tell him something though.

"I can arrange for a counselor to come talk to you, if you want. Help you deal with some of this."

"I don't think I'll need that."

"You will."

I shoot free throws most of the morning. It takes me at least half an hour to even get to the point where I'm starting to let go of my thoughts and feelings.

There's just too damned much in my head. Fear. Worry. Guilt. Helplessness.

It doesn't help that Agent Johnson waits around the three-point line the entire time. Watching. Checking angles and lines of sight.

Trying to decide where he would set up, if he were a sniper trying to take me down while I stood here trying to focus on my free-throw routine.

That's more than a little distracting.

Also, he's still certain I'm withholding information. He thinks it's because I'm scared of some stupid kid thing I did that is technically illegal, but so unimportant to the NSA that when he finds out what it is he and his team will laugh about it later over drinks.

They do that periodically. Share laughs over drinks about the things people feel the need to hide. Like the married minister who was worried about his gay porn collection because he had downloaded it all illegally.

Yeah, thanks Agent "Johnson." That was a mental image I didn't need.

Eventually though, my routine begins to combine with my firmly established habit of meditation, and everything begins to clear for me.

My body repeats the steps perfectly, each and every bounce and spin all the way through release.

And my mind finally empties.

At the moment of emptiness, there's always a sense of expansion. It's like...

Imagine all your thoughts and feelings and conflicts and worries and mental notes and reminder ticks and stress and strain and scheduling and more as the ripples in a tub full of bathwater.

Starting to meditate is pulling the drain. The chaos gets worse for a moment until it settles down into an orderly swirl.

Finally, the tub is empty. And that feels like it should be perfect. Complete.

But there's more.

Because once the tub is empty, the tub is no longer just a tub. It's the size of a kidney pool. Then it's the size of a regulation Olympic pool. Then an emptied lake.

And it just keeps expanding. As long as it stays empty.

But meditation isn't an end. It's a process. Thoughts keep coming at me, and if I let them catch my attention the tub starts shrinking again so it can fill.

The trick is to let them pass on through. Just slip down into the drain before they can accumulate.

Most days I can hold that state for quite some time. Long enough that I have to set an alarm so the day doesn't get away from me entirely.

Today is not one of those days.

Two thoughts keep coming back until they slam into me at the same time and form a connection I can't ignore.

If I'm unavailable as a target for too long, the assassin moves on to contingency targets.

My parents are back at work for a half-day.

CLANG!

"I was starting to think you don't miss," says Agent Johnson. "That was one hundred fifteen in a row by my count."

The ball bounces off toward the house. I just stare at it for a moment.

"I have to get out of here."

"Calm down." Agent Johnson's eyes scan the perimeter like he thinks I've heard gunfire. One hand goes to his ear, checking a report. "No hasty decisions. No rushing. Be smart and stay alive."

My guts are icy. Solid.

"You said it yourself. No deaths in a couple of days."

I look at Agent Johnson and I feel him respond to my distress.

The fear he sees in me. Fear that barely registers past the thick layer of shock that's wrapped me like a blanket for what feels like days now.

"What if there are contingency targets? I have to get out of here or that assassin might kill my parents."

Open hand slap across my face. Sharp. Pissing off my neck and shoulder muscles again.

It *does* root me back in the moment, though, listening to Agent Johnson's words.

"I get it," he says. "That was the fear talking. Living under a credible death threat isn't easy. People tend to either break down or step up. You want to step up. Face the threat and resolve it. That's admirable."

He grabs me by the chin.

"It's also stupid. Technically you may be an adult, but believe me. You're a kid, you're untrained, and you're in way over your head. You rush out of here you'll be dead before noon and nothing any of my people can do will stop that."

Now he's the one holding something back. I call him on it.

"You know who the killer is. Tell me."

"I'm not one hundred percent certain."

The name isn't there on the tip of his mind the way it should be. He's thinking about too many other things. Plans. Contingencies.

He's focusing like he's deliberately trying to hide the name.

But why would he do that?

Unless he knows what I am...

"I didn't want to say anything until I knew for sure."

He's stalling for time. Almost daring me to go into his head. To find the answers for myself.

All right, "Agent Johnson" aka Special Agent Colin McIntosh. You want me to go into your head for answers?

Maybe I should do just that.

Agent Johnson — or rather Special Agent Colin McIntosh, since I'm in his head I ought to use his proper name — has four other agents in the neighborhood right now. He has another one watching my parents and one more watching Tony.

He has another team of six in the East Bay right now, running down leads at the Port of Oakland, CalTrain stations, and a couple of car rental agencies.

His thoughts move in systematic, orderly ways, even here at the outer edges. They worry at gaps, like a tongue probing at a sore spot in his mouth.

But no matter how much attention he gives his plans, there's one element he can't leave out of his thoughts.

Me.

The nineteen-year-old standing in front of him, grandstanding past near-debilitating fear. But there's something else. Something familiar about me. Something that doesn't inspire trust...

I look off into the distance. A lot.

And I meditate. Daily.

The pieces didn't fall together for Special Agent McIntosh until he stood watching me shoot free throws for more than twenty minutes without missing.

It reminded him of Edwina.

Edwina, the skinny forty-something woman with streaks of gray in her flat brown hair and wrinkles around her eyes from too much sun and too little sleep. She always smelled like raisins and coconut oil.

Edwina is one of the remote viewers in that little red house in Alexandria, Virginia. Special Agent McIntosh saw her every day while he was working on that assignment.

Edwina was the one who convinced him there might be something to this Project Stargate after all. She told him how his house was getting robbed *while it was happening*.

The robber was caught. Everything returned. All because of Edwina.

And the first thing Edwina did every day before she started

"working" was meditate. She would bounce a red ball from a child's game of jacks and catch it. And while she did, she got the same faraway look I get when I shoot free throws. She never watched the ball. But she caught it exactly the same way every time.

And now Special Agent McIntosh thinks I'm a remote viewer too.

And he's holding back information to see how long it takes me to tip my hand. He thinks I may have done it already. I didn't react hard enough to the news of Stephen's death. Like I already knew about it.

Which I did, of course.

But I've also suffered so many shocks lately that the Special Agent can't be sure I'm not just getting numb.

Which is also true, if I'm honest. I'm not sure how much more of this I can take.

That's why he's holding back the name of the killer. He wants to see if I find it out myself. He wants to let me go out into the world. Thinks that my "gift" will help his men keep me safe. Thinks we can take down the killer today. If we do it right.

The name is right there for the taking. Just behind a wall of surface thoughts. So many links to it I couldn't miss it if I tried.

Not just the name either. I can tell without going deeper. Practically a dossier here in Special Agent McIntosh's mind. Just waiting for me to open it up and dig out a few details.

I want to do it.

I want to get this over with. End the threat. Even at the risk of my anonymity.

But I pull back from his mind instead.

BACK IN MY OWN HEAD NOW.

I'm standing on the basketball court beside my parent's converted garage, face to face with Agent "Johnson." I can smell Mom's hydrangeas beside the garage. I can hear distant lawnmowers and the rustling of a cool summer breeze.

My hands expect the basketball to be between them, but it's still off on the grass to one side after that last miss.

My stomach remains a cold pit of fear that while Agent Johnson is playing information games, a killer might be lining up a shot at *my parents.*

"I'm not the press," I say. My words slow and heavy. "I'm not an attorney, or a judge, or your superior at work. I'm just the kid whose life is in your hands.

"And I'm scared. All right? I'm so scared I can hardly sleep or eat. Last night I collapsed unconscious beside my toilet because I kept throwing up. From fear."

I start rubbing the knots in my shoulders and neck.

"I know you guys are doing your best to keep me safe. But right now, all I know is there's a professional killer coming after me. Someone so good you guys haven't caught him yet. Or her, maybe, I don't know.

"This is some serious bogeyman shit. Give me a name to focus on. A face. Something. Something to keep me from falling prey to movie clichés."

Agent Johnson blinks. Only once, but it's enough.

"Come on inside. Let's talk."

I start to move after my basketball, but he says, "Leave it for now. It'll be all right."

We go back through the side door and into the kitchen, where Agent Johnson gets me a glass of tap water before he joins me at the table.

"You're a smart kid, Rick. Do you mind if I call you Rick?"

"You're trying to keep me alive. Call me whatever you want."

"Rick it is." Agent Johnson drums his middle finger on the red oak of the kitchen table for a moment. "Now you're a smart kid, but smart kids sometimes get killed faster than dumb ones. Do you know why that is?"

"Smart kids think they know what they're doing, but dumb ones know they don't know?"

"Something like that." He drums that finger again. "As of this morning, I've narrowed it down to two possible killers. If I give you a name or a face, you're going to get on your computer or tablet or whatever and research the person trying to kill you, right?"

"Duh."

He snorts at my Captain Obvious expression.

"And if that killer has figured out how to hack the device?"

That makes me sit straighter.

"Is that a possibility?"

"Depends on how good you are at setting passwords and how determined your would-be killer is to see your online pictures of your breakfast."

"I don't— Oh that was just an example."

Agent Johnson nods.

"So don't tell me name and face. But tell me something."

That earns me a raised eyebrow.

Damn it. He was just about to suggest that. And he has enough suspicions playing through his mind that he won't care that I happened to get there on my own.

And it's not like I can tell him.

"There are six known hitters who could accomplish what this one has so far. One of them refuses to use sniper rifles as a matter of personal principal. Two more have been spotted in Europe in the last three days. The fourth is currently serving time for tax evasion.

"That leaves two solid possibilities. One male, one female. Both in their mid-thirties. Both American, though the woman has ties to the IRA."

Agent Johnson looks me dead in the eye and thinks hard about a name.

I catch what he's doing and bite the inside of my cheek to shift focus away from him.

Too late.

The name he's thinking is Karen Muldoon. She's a petite redhead who might look pretty except she always has an angry expression.

"I'm waiting for some intel from INTERPOL to confirm a couple of things. I should have a better idea of whom we're dealing with by…

"What's wrong, Rick?"

Bit my cheek too hard. I can taste blood. Feel the wince on my face. The squeeze of my eyes.

"We'll stop this person, Rick. *Whoever* it is."

"But what if..." my words run together a bit because I don't want to open my mouth. "But what if there *is* a contingency plan? What if the killer has other targets, in case I go into hiding?"

"That would take a lot of forethought."

"You said the killer was planning around your presence. Why then not—"

"That kind of planning is the killer's job. Contingency targets would mean serious planning by the payer. And enough extra money to..."

Thoughts coming together in his head. I focus on the throb in my cheek and the leftover kink in my neck to keep from reading him.

"Your boy Stephen DeFaustino. Had to be him." Agent Johnson jumps to his feet. "Don't leave this table. I'll be back in five. Then we can talk about your hike."

Agent Johnson is out the side door and into the yard, talking on his phone.

I don't care what he's saying though. I have something more important to look into.

—*Hey.*— I send into the shocked mind of Tony. But before he can reply, I say, —*I only have a sec. But I need you to dig up everything you can on a Karen Muldoon.*—

—*Agent Johnson is sure she's our killer.*—

11

———

Hillside Mall.

A three story suburban complex, that stretches across Camino Grande, the major street along here.

Acres of floor space devoted to capitalism: department stores, boutiques, specialty shops, kiosks, and a bowling alley/pool hall converted from the old ice skating rink.

There's no hillside, despite the name. The nearest rise in the ground that might be called a hill is a good five hundred yards past the far edge of the parking lot.

Speaking of the parking lot, it's nearly full. Not bad, since last year this time it only got about half-full. Good sign for our area's economy.

I don't know what it is about this mall, but to me it always smells like a carnival just left: old popcorn and hot dogs, with a hint of sugary snacks. It's true in the parking lot, and it's true in the food court.

The food court is where I am right now, sitting on a hard plastic chair, across a hard plastic table from Tony.

That we have a table at all draws some stink eye from the lunchtimers, who move slowly past holding their trays with expressions of expectation. That the table is in the center of the food court seems to irritate them even more.

That we don't even have drinks appears to be the ultimate indignity.

But I don't really care what they think.

The food court here is circular and under a dome of tiered glass. It's bright. It's clear, and Tony and I can see unimpeded in each direction as far as the food joints or the place the food court rejoins the mall itself.

In other words, I feel safe here. Like we can see every angle.

And the fact that this provides ample opportunity for us to enjoy the sights of the girls in their airy summer outfits doesn't hurt.

Also, the dull roar of enthusiastic conversation punctuated by the complaints of children covers our discussion.

"I can't find anything about a Karen Muldoon," says Tony.

"Nothing?"

"Well, I can find out more than you ever wanted to know about more Karen Muldoons than you would ever have suspected exist. Including one who's a model, and well worth looking at. But nothing that suggests that any of them are assassins."

"No ties to the IRA?"

"Oh, plenty of Karen Muldoons there too. But I didn't dig into that too much." Tony chuckles. "Wouldn't look good for a boy from a nice German family to start doing research into *Sinn Fein*."

"Shoot. I was hoping for at least some newspaper clippings or something."

"Would that help you connect to her mind?"

"No, but it would help me spot her if she wandered through the mall right now."

Tony and I both stop and look around. Neither of us sees a likely Karen Muldoon, though Tony does enjoy the sight of a young mother leaning down to strap her baby back into its stroller.

"So how's Sabrina?" I ask, innocently.

"Don't change the subject," he says, eyes still on the young mother. When he does turn back to me, he says, "So Project Stargate is a real thing?"

"Now who's changing the subject?"

"What are we doing here, Rick?" Tony cranes his neck to look around again. "You couldn't possibly be more exposed than you are right now."

"Actually, this was the safest place I could think of." My turn to let my eyes flit about. "I never come here."

"Apart from the view, there's nothing to..." He raps his knuckles on the table. "And the others were all killed when they were someplace they went all the time."

"Exactly."

"So what, though? I mean, yippee, you're safe here at the mall. But we're still at the mall."

"So," I say sliding him a five. "You're going to get us a couple of sodas. Then you're going to keep an eye on me while I do some telepathic heavy lifting."

"I am?"

"Yep. Because the chances are pretty good that our Ms. Muldoon is here somewhere, studying her target.

"And I think it's time for the hunter to become the hunted."

AT THE BALLPARK I WAS ABLE TO RIDE THE JOY AND TENSION OF FORTY thousand attentive minds. At most games a good-sized portion of the crowd would have been distracted, but this was the Giants against the Dodgers. Almost everyone was paying attention, either to the game or to the ballpark experience.

It was a rush.

In fact, I wish I were doing it right now.

Because sifting through the distracted thoughts of some thousand-plus mall shoppers is much, much more difficult.

But because I'm thinking of that ballgame a couple of days ago, the first thing I try to do is find the gestalt.

I talk sometimes about white thought, or thought static, when it comes to crowds. That's what happens when the fog of thoughts from one person bumps up against the fog from another person. The more people, the more static. Pack an elevator with a panicked crowd and the static could overwhelm me.

Space everyone out though, and it feels less abrasive.

And if feels even less abrasive when the fogs share common elements. That is when a gestalt is formed. Instead of clashing, a gestalt is a sort of thought-resonance.

It connects concepts and ideas and gives them harmony.

That's what I want to find right now.

Because enough people must be here focused on shopping and eating to bring one together.

I start by letting myself ease into the surface thoughts that surround me.

Rude punks holding a prime table when they aren't even—
I can't believe she got that shade of pink. It would go perfect with my—
Whoa-ho-ho, watch that bounce, baby, you could put an eye—
Six dollars for this? I remember when it would have cost—

Shoot. I shouldn't have tried this in the food court. I should have started in a department store or something. I can't find two minds in a row going the same direction. Nothing but chaos here. No gestalt to ride.

So what *can* I do?

Well, I'm sitting here, out in the open. If Muldoon is here, her mind should be somewhere nearby. And thinking about me...

This time as my thoughts move out, it's like I'm playing a big game of duck-duck-goose. I spiral out from my table, touching every mind I come to just long enough to get a sense of identity and focus, then move on.

Guy tearing into his chili cheese fries. Duck.

Girl sharing a pretzel with her best friend. Duck.

Man wrangling three children around a table full of chicken parts. Duck.

And outward I go, spiraling through the minds first of the diners around me, then further out into the food court, and finally into the mall itself.

Woman thinking about the skimpy panties she just bought and how awesome they will feel during the big meeting. Duck.

Boy sighing wistfully over the price of a signed Jerry Rice jersey, torn between admiration and desire. Duck.

Woman, wondering angrily what the hell I'm doing here and how much longer she'll have to—

Goose.

No. Wait. Duck.

This is Agent Ariana Templeton, who hates this assignment and hates politicos who have the pull to drag up-and-coming field agents off of important duties to play bodyguard for a spoiled brat who drives a kit car that costs more than her—

I don't think I need to follow the rest of this.

I keep going, sifting through more nearby minds.

Girl who kissed her best friend's boyfriend at a party and is trying to figure out how to tell her. Duck.

Boy, who only needs one more *Game of Thrones* figure to complete his set, if he can find it. Duck.

Man, who is thinking about angles and whether or not I will be sitting here long enough for him to close for a better shot.

Goose.

THE KILLER'S THOUGHTS ARE SO SIMPLE AND BRUTAL THAT I'M SHOCKED into looking at him. Here in my own body in the middle of the busy food court.

I whip my head around, painfully re-kinking my neck, and stare across the mall and into the eyes of a man in his forties. No more than twenty yards from me. He's big. Like he played halfback in college or something. Short, dark black hair. Nondescript gray suit and tie.

Big hands. One of which is reaching into his jacket when I meet his eyes.

I feel his shock across the room.

He swears and pulls something out of his jacket.

Not a gun. A grenade.

He throws it and runs.

I yank our table over, ducking behind it. I'm screaming for Tony to get down. People are staring. Someone laughs.

And then the grenade goes off.

A flash of light. A boom shakes the table. Smoke.

My ears ring. Tony's next to me.

Must have gotten down. Good for him.

He's saying something, but I can't hear him. And neither can he. He's trying to ask me if that was the killer. I'll tell him later.

Right now I'm reaching for a killer's mind.

And not finding it.

I slump down against the table. Commotion all around me, but I can't hear it. Tony's looking at me. Scared. I am too, but by this point I'm more pissed off than scared.

I had him. I had the bastard. I went looking for his mind and I found it.

And because he wasn't a woman I got shocked back into my own head.

I never got a fix on him. I never had a moment of solid enough contact to get a real feel for his mind. Sure, I'll recognize his thoughts again if I find him again. But I can't just reach out to him no matter where he goes.

Not like I could have done if I'd taken just a moment longer. I wouldn't have even had to thrust deep into his thoughts. I just needed to give myself a moment to adjust. To get the feel of his head.

But no. I couldn't do it. I expected to find a woman and found a man and couldn't adjust fast enough.

A woman in front of me now. Agent Templeton. Her mind I could find again.

"...hear me." Her words are distant. Tony's shaking his head, but I can make out what she's saying under a thick layer of high-pitched whine. "We need to get you out of here. Now."

"My car is—"

She winces like I'm yelling. I probably am.

"Not your car. My car. No debate. Now."

She pulls us to our feet and my guilt spikes higher than ever. Because now I can see all the people who weren't behind a table when the grenade went off.

People crying and holding each other and clutching their ears. Adults and teenagers and children alike.

Fear. Pain. As far as I can see.

Some people are running, but most of them are wide-eyed and huddling.

No one dead. That's something. Must have been a flash-bang. No serious concussion or fragmentation.

But people are hurt. And they're hurt because I fucked up. Because I wasn't together enough to deal with the unexpected.

Agent Templeton has her gun out and low. With her other hand she grips my plain gray tee shirt at the shoulder. Tony's just a step behind me.

She doesn't take us into the mall. Instead she pushes between mini-restaurants and into the employee-only area. We're through a door and into a hall covered in time sheets and legally posted notices about labor laws and practices.

A couple of guys in yellow clown tops whistle like Tony and I are in trouble. I barely hear them over the ringing in my ears.

But Agent Templeton moves with authority and certainty. No one questions her.

No one but me.

"But the killer—"

"The guy was a decoy. And he's already down." She pauses and looks me dead in the eye. "No more questions. I have to get you home in one piece. No one said you have to be conscious when you get there. Got me?"

I raise my hands in surrender.

THE SECOND I'M INSIDE OUR FRONT DOOR MY MOM HAS ME WRAPPED IN a hug so tight I can't breathe. Tony tries to slip into the house around me, and Mom lets go exactly far enough so she can pull him into the hug.

"You almost died," she says as she finally eases back. "I would never have forgiven myself."

Dad gives us each a hug too, but he doesn't try to crack our rib cages.

"You should be proud of your boy," says Agent Johnson from a few steps behind my dad. "I understand the second he saw a weapon he dove for cover and tried to pull Tony down with him."

Mom smiles, but it doesn't wipe the fear or the tears from her face. Dad gives me a smile that shows more pride. But then, if he's been crying you wouldn't know it to look at him.

"And now that they *are* safe at home," says Agent Johnson, "I need to talk to these boys."

Mom starts to lead me over to the leather sectional.

"You can, of course, stay if you wish." Agent Johnson's tone makes it clear that he hopes they won't. "But the questions I have to ask them may be difficult for them to answer in front of you two."

"Nonsense," says Dad. "We're honest with each other in this family."

"And I'm sure then that Rick will tell you everything later. But time is of the essence here, and I need to make sure they don't hesitate to admit some truth that might be embarrassing."

Mom and Dad look at each other, uncertain.

"Please," said Agent Johnson. "They'll be right here, safe as kittens."

Mom and Dad protest a little more, but give us the living room. Tony and I grab seats on the leather sectional, while Agent Johnson sits at the front edge of a recliner.

I start trying again to rub that kink away.

"I'm glad you boys are safe. Let's be clear about that." He leans forward a little more. "Now what the hell were you playing at? You went to a mall, but didn't go to any stores? You went to the food court and didn't eat?"

"It's the best place in town for girl watching. Rick's been cooped up for days."

"Rick is getting calls from Isla Perkins. I don't think he needs—"

"No shit?" Tony's eyebrows threaten to merge with his mass of curls. "And I was going to hear about this when?"

"The last few days have been kind of crazy."

"Not enough excuse for this."

"ENOUGH."

Agent Johnson waits until we're both looking at him to continue.

"Now don't bullshit me, boys. Neither one of you has the life experience to pull it off. Rick, what the hell was the point of today's little excursion?"

"I had to get out of the house. I was going stir crazy." I run my hands through my hair. Let my head hang forward a little to stretch my neck. "I was going to go for a hike, but I couldn't."

I look up at Agent Johnson.

"I *go* for hikes. It's one of the things I love to do. And Jamal and Mary and Darcy? They were all killed doing things they loved to do. Going places they went all the time."

"Smart," says Agent Johnson with a nod. "So you just wanted someplace the two of you could talk. Someplace you don't go often, but should be safe enough."

"And I was wrong about that." Weariness and bitterness all through my tone.

"You say that, but you're still alive. Don't let that escape your notice."

"Lots of people were hurt."

"And almost all of them will recover."

Agent Johnson snaps his fingers to get me to look at him.

"What happened in that mall is not your fault. You didn't make that man throw a flash-bang. He did it because you saw him before he could take his shot.

"Speaking of which." Agent Johnson tilts his head and lowers his eyebrows. "Agent Templeton says you whirled around and looked at him all of a sudden. Just how did you know to do that?"

Tony tries to pretend he's not here.

"An ... itch between my shoulder blades?"

Even I don't think I sound convinced of that.

"Uh huh. And tell me, Tony, how is it you came to start running web searches today looking for a Karen Muldoon?"

"I heard about this model—"

"Save it." Agent Johnson sighs deep and heavy. "Look, Rick. I've got some experience with people like you. Just enough to know the signs and know it isn't bullshit.

"But remember something. I'm not here officially. Anything I learn about you while I'm here trying to *save your life* doesn't ever have to go into any reports. It can be our little secret."

"You said your presence here may yet become official." My tone is flat as a punctured basketball. "So I'm afraid I don't know what you're talking about."

Tony stares at me, wide-eyed. He can't believe how close I just came to an admission.

"Fair enough." Agent Johnson nods, then snorts with a smile. "I did say you were smart." He drums one finger on the recliner. "How about this then? You don't tell me anything. Not directly. And in return, I don't notice anything you can do, even if my presence here becomes official.

"And in the meantime, you just tell me how I can help you do ... whatever it is you do. And you share with me any information you ... gather. That way we're not working against each other, and our chances of keeping you alive go up. Which I assume we both want?"

Agent Johnson extends his hand to me.

I nod as I shake it.

"All right." He stands up. "I'll leave two alone for a few minutes so you can collate whatever it is you've figured out with your little exper-iment today. And when you're ready, you and I can have another talk."

Agent Johnson leaves the room.

Tony turns to me.

"Did he mean what he said?"

"He meant it," I say with a nod. "He wants this over with. He wants us all safe. He wants to take down this killer. And he wants to get his teams back on their regular work."

Tony looks off down the hall where Agent Johnson went.

"And if he changes his mind?"

I chuckle.

"Then I'll make sure he doesn't."

INTERLUDE TWO

Transcription of a brief telepathic exchange between Rick Blackhall and Tony Gottschalk.

Rick: He doesn't actually know about my telepathy.

Tony: But he—

Rick: He thinks I'm a remote viewer. Thinks I got the name Karen Muldoon from the notebook in his pocket. He planted it atop a list of suspects as a false lead.

Tony: He keeps an actual notebook in this day and age?

Rick: He can tear and eat or burn paper quickly.

Tony: ...This guy seems pretty serious, Rick. Are you sure you want to trust him?

Rick: Not sure I have much choice. Talk to you tomo—

Tony: Wait! ... Seriously? Isla Perkins wants a date?

Rick: It's just a friendly dinner. I caught a problem early for her.

Tony: Look, you blew it with Candi. Do not blow it with Isla. You owe this to your gender. You—

Rick: Catch you later, Tony.

12

———

It's close to midnight again, and I'm trying to sleep. I'm naked at least, instead of fully clothed like last night. And I ate dinner tonight. Chicken Alfredo with asparagus and hollandaise sauce, and some very good garlic bread.

So that's something. Even if it is all sitting together like a rock in my stomach.

And I'm under the fresh-smelling sheets of my pillow-top queen-sized bed tonight instead of lying on top of the bedspread.

Either way, I'm still staring up at where my ceiling would be if I could see it through the darkness.

Nothing breaking the blackness except the L.E.D.s of various power supplies around the room.

And the clock. In case I want to know exactly how close to midnight it is.

I don't.

My pounding heart says it doesn't matter anyway.

Agent Johnson seems excited about our plan. He honestly believes it will work. And he's the one who should know. The one with the experience. The one who has done this sort of thing for years.

He knows what he's doing.

I should trust him.

So why don't I?

I suppose it could be because it's my life on the line, not his. Or maybe it's just because I've never done this before myself.

Fact number one: the assassin will not try to strike while I am holed up in my house. I have to get out there and make myself a target or this is my life from here on out. Because...

Fact number two: the assassin will not go away. A million dollars is a lot of money. Well worth riding out the summertime waiting. Waiting for me to go back to Cal this fall and provide an easy target.

Fact number three: in the meantime, people I love will die. Stephen was telling the truth about that. There's a contingency clause in the contract and a second account. I saw it in his head. If I hide out here too long, the assassin will move on my parents, Tony, Jenna, Candi, even Amaris for good measure.

Not that I'm saying I love Amaris. I mean, that's over.

And Candi's just a friend. She's made that clear enough.

And Jenna, well, Jenna's complicated.

I slap myself across the face to stop *that* spiral. The last thing I need on my mind right now is girls. I can worry about them when I survive this thing.

If I survive it.

The point is, these are people I care about and I can't let them get killed while I hide out in my house.

So I have to go out there tomorrow and risk my own death to try to keep them alive.

And all because no one knows which of two killers is after me, or where to find either of them. One of Agent Johnson's teams has been tearing the Bay Area apart for more than a day now, but leads keep evaporating.

They have proven Stephen was involved, but not beyond a reasonable doubt. They found evidence of the transfer out of his accounts of more than five million dollars.

A million for each of the telepaths who ejected Stephen from their number, plus some change to close out any "necessary" loved ones.

The transfer doesn't prove where the money went or why. If Stephen were still alive, he might claim it was a tax sheltering move, and plead down to a tax evasion charge or less.

Stephen. The man I killed. That thought is enough to make me nauseous, and I lie there panting shallow breaths until it passes. It had to be done. I'm sure of it.

And I tell myself that over and over for longer than I'd like to contemplate.

Finally, I get back on point.

Stephen doesn't matter. I can face what I did to him later. Right now only the assassin matters.

Stephen is gone, but the assassin is still out there.

I have information from Agent Johnson about the two possibilities now. He's hoping I can use my knack to find them both. Figure out where they are and which is involved, so he can send his men there first thing in the morning.

Clean the whole mess up with no more threat to anyone.

Only one problem.

I can't do that.

If I actually were a remote viewer, maybe I could. Maybe I could take this image Darla Swenson and the profile of her time in the Swiss Special Forces and the detailed but incomplete history of her move to mercenary work and finally assassination and "get a fix" on her.

But to me she just looks like a blonde with hard, angry features and more muscles than I have. And a scar along her chin.

But honestly, it wouldn't matter if he gave me her full psych profile and a videotaped interview. I need a hook into her mind, not her face or body.

I can't just stare at a picture and connect to someone. Not if I've never met them, either through my own mind or someone else's.

So I can't find Darla Swenson. And I can't find Alonso Gutierrez either. Gutierrez is razor blade thin with a pencil-thin mustache, and caramel skin that has never come near a tattoo needle.

He's never been in the military either, though he's been in and out of prison his whole life.

He never had any formal training, but he's a hell of a sharp-shooter. His rep says he can put out the eye of a sparrow at two hundred paces with a .22.

Agent Johnson expects me to have good news for him in the morning. He expects me to be able to tell him which one is the killer. Maybe even where said killer is hiding.

Agent Johnson even gave me the found shell casing from the Desert Eagle used to kill Mary. Just in case it helps.

And I can't just tell him that this isn't what I do. Because it's bad enough that Agent Johnson even knows I have a knack. A psychic gift.

While he thinks I'm a remote viewer he thinks I'm a known quantity. Understandable. That I'm like his Edwina.

But Agent Johnson has never met a telepath, as far as he knows. That means I'm something "new." Something the government might not even know is out there.

I'm a mind reader. And my parents put me in a position to meet diplomats, dignitaries and more.

That makes me a major security risk. *If* Agent Johnson finds out.

So Agent Johnson can't find out. Or that deal might be off. Or he might disappear me. Maybe Terrence too, because Agent Johnson already suspects our little group was all remote viewers.

I have to come up with something to tell him in the morning. Something believable, so he doesn't suspect the truth.

Worse, the safest version of our plan involves my finding the assassin long before I end up in his or her sights.

That's not possible either.

So I just lie here awake, on what might be my last night on this earth.

And instead of thinking about good things, I have to figure out how to tell a believable lie to someone who spots lies for a living.

And then, oh, yeah, survive an attempt by a professional assassin.
Little red digits tell me it's midnight now.
Gonna be a long night.

13

———

AROUND SIX IN THE MORNING I PUT ON MY WORN OLD RED ROBE AND drag myself downstairs.

I've got that strung-out feeling all through my muscles. Like they want to ache, but they just don't have the energy. My head feels a step behind the world. Like I move my arm so my hand is on the banister, and a moment later I'm still feeling my arm move.

My steps feel flat and lifeless.

I can smell coffee in the kitchen, but my nostrils can't be bothered to flare any interest. My stomach rumbles that it's empty and angry at me for taking more ibuprofen without eating anything.

I promise it food, but it doesn't believe me.

I shuffle into the kitchen where Agent Johnson is gathered around the kitchen table with Agent Templeton and two other agents I haven't officially met yet.

I can feel them discussing the day's plans, even though they stop talking when I come into the room. They're all thinking about sight lines and bullet velocity and things like that.

I grunt out a greeting and head for the cabinet where we keep the mugs.

"Did you get any sleep at all?" asks Agent Johnson while his compatriots clear out of the room.

I shake my head and pour the coffee. My teaspoon clinks against the side of the cup as I stir in fake sugar, to keep the acid from eating its way down through my guts. My stomach is mad enough as it is.

Says something about how much I need the caffeine that I'm willing to drink coffee at all.

"That's not good. Maybe you should take some Benadryl and have a nap."

I sip. The brew is strong and bitter. Could have used another teaspoon of fake sugar. I sip again before I say anything.

"I managed a few minutes here and there. It'll have to do. Can't be drugged while I'm out there."

"No," he says slowly, "I suppose not. Any luck with—"

I start shaking my head again and Agent Johnson's mouth stretches into a line.

"I was afraid of that. You're too close to it. Aren't you?"

I nod, thinking that sounds much better than the crap excuse I'd cobbled together about astral tides or something.

He sighs heavily.

"That's how it is for the others I've known. I knew a guy who could tell you what a Russian sub commander had for breakfast deep in the Indian Ocean, but not that his wife was cheating on him every Tuesday for five years. I guess it doesn't work if you care too much about the results."

I sip again to keep from tipping how this is the first I've heard of anything like this.

Heck, for me the more personal it is, the harder a time I have *not* finding out what I need to know.

At least, as long as I'm in close proximity to the information. I mean, right now Tony could be having a deep, important conversation with his fiancé Sabrina in which they make all the big decisions in my life and I'd never know it. Not unless I happened to reach for one of their minds at the right time.

"Tell me again how the plan works," he says. "In your own words."

I sigh, but at least I can feel the caffeine begin to perk me up a bit.

"I drive myself out to Mission Trail State Park. It's early and a weekday, so I should have a good selection of parking spots. I'll park under the boulder if I can, so I'm protected from deeper into the park by the boulder in front of me and the wall of sequoias everywhere else.

"I hike trail number three for two hours out. Take a break at my usual trail three clearing and eat my lunch. Then two hours back.

"During the hike there will be three major points of exposure. As I pass each I drop something and bend to pick it up without stopping.

"At no point do I look around for the killer or for your men. If all goes according to plan, you'll apprehend the assassin without my noticing. If that happens, you'll call me on my cell."

I grab a cinnamon raisin bagel and slice it.

"And if anything goes wrong?" he asks.

"If anything goes wrong, you'll text me 911 and I'm to drop to the ground and hide until you come get me."

"Keep your head down and covered. Put your watch in your pocket. Move as little as possible. Any kind of movement or reflection could tip your location."

I drop the bagel in the toaster and turn to the fridge for butter.

"Are you sure I shouldn't wear a vest for this?"

"Just like I told your parents, there are two reasons you shouldn't." He holds up a finger. "One, under one of your concert tee shirts it would look like a floatation device."

He holds up a second finger, and locks eyes with me.

"I told your parents the second reason was that we plan on keeping the killer from ever taking a shot. And that's true. We will do our best to keep you from ever being under direct threat. But that's not the real reason we don't want to bother with a vest."

He takes a deep breath, but I can already feel the answer floating in the air around him. And I'm tired enough that I say it first.

"Vests aren't made to stop fifty caliber rounds from a sniper rifle."

"The bullet would punch right through it. Wouldn't even slow down appreciably."

I'm still staring at the butter when the bagel pops up.

A HALF-DOZEN CARS IN THE PARKING LOT. ANY ONE OF THEM COULD belong to the assassin. Mostly SUVs, plus a couple of sedans and a station wagon that looks old enough to remember the Nixon administration.

The back of my neck itches. A bullet could come from anywhere. Right now.

I'm still parked under the boulder in my Fiberfab Valkyrie. At least, if there's a chase scene, my car is up to the task. Be the first time the speedometer passed seventy in almost a year.

The image of the horrified look that fact would put on Tony's face makes me smile. Gives me enough courage to get out of the car.

There's a picnic area just short of the wall of sequoias to my right. Twelve benches and eight small barbecues, plus the restroom building.

Three people nearby me. A woman tightening the laces on her running shoes. She's got spandex on and wavy chestnut hair wrangled into a ponytail.

If she's hiding a weapon, she's doing a good job of it.

There's a sloppy looking guy over by the benches, like he's lost in a shirt and shorts combo that's way too big for him, and he misplaced his comb and razor while trying to find his way out.

But he's smiling, and he's got a pair of Dobies and a German shepherd on leashes who look as though today is the most absolutely fantastic day they could ever have conceived of and they're just happy to be a part of it.

I have to admit, they have a point. The sky is clear and pale blue. The air is still cool from last night, and the scent of forest is almost enough to send a wave of relaxation through those rocks I think of as my shoulder muscles.

The last person nearby is a serious hiker. He has on trail boots, a short-sleeved green plaid flannel shirt, and khaki shorts with more than their share of pockets. He's filling an actual canteen. One of those round kind that you wear on a strap.

He's got a boot knife, and a utility knife, but his thoughts are all about the park. This is a man with a plan, and he intends to cover every foot of every trail and still be home in time for dinner.

Now that's what I call regimented fun. But at least he's not a killer either. Unless you count small game animals.

He's better prepared than I am, though, in my plaid shorts, plain green shirt, and hiking sandals. I've got a couple of bottles of water and a peanut butter sandwich in my small backpack, but that's about it.

Oh, and a Swiss army knife, which might be ironic, depending on who it is exactly who's trying to kill me.

No one else nearby. Unless you count my trail car. But they won't pull in from the road until I get onto the trail.

So I guess it's time to stop delaying.

And so I hike.

ABOUT FORTY-FIVE MINUTES LATER I'M APPROACHING THE FIRST DANGER spot. There's a break in the sequoias and attendant foliage on my left that has clear visibility for at least a half-mile.

Long enough to make a sniper feel comfortable.

There's been no one else on the trail with me. No early risers coming back. No joggers pushing past me. No one.

I can't hear anything but the birds singing.

No minds anywhere near me except animals. Squirrels. A couple of raccoons. Those singing birds.

But no human beings.

Coincidence? Or the work of Agent Johnson's people?

Doesn't matter.

Stop delaying, Rick. You need to cross the break point.

The sweat is cold on my face, and more dampens all the joins on my body. My heart is pounding. Wants me to speed up. Just run past the danger zone.

But that's not the plan.

Just as well. My legs still feel like lead.

So I close my eyes and try not to feel like a target in a shooting gallery.

I count my steps, which come on every fifth heartbeat. I feel the press of my sandals into the dirt trail and listen to their slight crunch and scrape with each step.

Warming sunlight on my face tells me when I reach the break. I lean down like I'm picking up a stick in passing.

I clench my teeth hard to keep them from chattering. My bladder wants to let go. I'm breathing hard enough to inflate an Olympic-sized swimming pool.

But then I feel shadow on my face once more. I'm past the danger zone and I just collapse forward onto the dirt path, barely catching myself on my hands.

Tears are running down my face, but I don't even feel like I'm crying anymore. I don't feel anything at all. I'm just too tired and scared. My heart is still pounding, and I feel light-headed.

I try to slow it all down. One breath at a time. Deep in. Hold. Slow out. Hold.

Deep in. Hold. Slow out. Hold.

Deep in. Hold. Slow out. Hold.

Over and over. Just me on my hands and knees on a dirt path, staring at a tiny round pebble like it's the light that dead people see.

I keep my whole attention on that pebble until my breathing is something close to normal. My heart's still going too fast, but now it's nervous fast, not I'm-about-to-die fast.

I don't want to go anywhere. I just want to lie down here in the dirt for a while. No one else is around. There's no clear shot line. This may be the safest I can be outside my house.

But I can't do that. If I don't reach the next danger zone by the time Johnson's people expect me, they'll go all code red or something.

Then they'll be looking for me and not the person who wants to kill me. Or who is at least getting paid to kill me. Want might not enter into it.

Though that's an interesting question.

No, Rick. No more interesting questions. Get your ass up and get walking.

Each of us has his job to do in life. And right now, mine is getting to that next danger zone in fifteen minutes or less.

And as jobs go. This sucks.

NOTHING.

Today, I damn near gave myself stroke-level stress for ... nothing.

No attempts were made on my way out. Not at any one of the three danger zones. I sat and ate my "lunch" on a fairly comfortable bench under a clear blue sky at just short of ten in the morning.

The birds were serenading me. The squirrels were chittering and barking for crusts from my peanut butter sandwich.

And I couldn't enjoy the taste or smell of my lunch. I couldn't relax to the strains of the birds, or smile at the scent of summer roses growing in the relative wild.

I couldn't enjoy any of it because I was sweating and shaking over what felt like three near-death experiences, with three more to come on the walk back.

And all that stress to no good effect.

The shot was never fired.

I'm back in my car now, in the parking lot, which is mostly full around me. There must be twenty people between the parking lot and the picnic area, but none of them are thinking about killing me so I don't care who they are or what they want in life.

All I want to do is sleep.

All the stress and exhaustion is catching up with me. I'm not a hundred percent sure I'm safe to drive. I've got that half-unconscious nod going.

I'm tempted to just lean my seat back and catch a nap, but if that got me killed I think my parents would never forgive me.

So I start my car, and I put the windows down in my little sports kit-car to get as much fresh air on my face as I can. Anything to keep my eyes open a little longer.

The curves in the road out to the freeway help. Though they do give me that half-step-behind feeling again.

But that's all right. I may not be Tony, but my body knows how to drive on autopilot.

So I make it safely out to 280 North, where having my windows down means stirring more life into me at sixty-five miles per hour.

It helps that I have no blind spots. Even half-asleep I know where every mind around me is. Which means I pick up on a stranger's shock when I weave a little in my lane, and there's no risk of my failing to see someone and just plowing into them.

Well, let's be honest. *Almost* no risk.

I'm halfway to my exit when the phone rings.

"I'm sorry," I say as I answer hands-free, "Rick Blackhall is asleep right now. But if you'll leave a message—"

"Funny," says Agent Johnson in monotone. "Do you need to pull over and have one of my people drive you?"

"No, I've got it. I've driven this enough times that I could make it in my actual sleep, not just—"

"I'm not looking for jokes. And I'm worried about the other drivers as much as I am you."

"I'm fine. I swear."

"All right, but if you hit so much as a curb you're done driving until this is all over."

He cuts the line. I reach out to crank up my stereo, but I just can't bring myself to do it. Music has always been such a happy thing for me, and right now I feel anything but happy.

Well, that's not strictly true. I don't feel much of anything, including happy.

But even if I had a whole catalog of songs for every emotion, I doubt I could find one to cover me right now. I just don't have the emotional bandwidth.

But I make it to the Forest Road exit in one piece, without hitting so much as a curb.

I'm on autopilot as I pull off Forest Road into a little shopping center at the corner of Vine.

Not exactly a big, fancy place, and it's only a quarter-full today. Long Pine Savings and Loan looks like it has maybe three customers inside. Two storefronts up for lease. One closed, with a coming soon sign I can't be bothered to read.

Kim's Laundry has a couple of customers, but Dirk's Donuts is closed after the morning work rush. Most of the cars in the lot congregate near Crazy Zane's Food and Drug.

None of those places matter, though. I'm looking for Boomer's. Not for their coffee. For my green tea smoothie. A post-hike tradition ingrained so deeply into my bones that my body took me here even though there's nothing I want more than a nap.

My phone rings as I slide into a parking space six spots from the Boomer's door. I ignore it. I didn't hit anybody, Agent Johnson. Now let me get my smoothie in peace.

I lock the car and get out.

I take maybe two steps before I hear a car engine gunning my way. Blaring its horn.

I turn to see what the commotion is.

And my left shoulder explodes.

14

———

I'm spinning. And falling.

My left shoulder is on fire. So much pain. So much blood.

Another sound. Like a hammer blow cracking concrete.

No. Wait. I'm on concrete. I'm on the red sidewalk ... somewhere. Crying. And screaming. My right hand is covered in blood as I clutch my left shoulder. Or where my left shoulder should be, anyway.

Hardly feels like it's still there.

The pain is though.

The pain is everywhere. Through my teeth and head. All the way down to my balls. Even my feet. Not fair.

Most of all in my shoulder. Feels like half of it is missing and the rest is jagged. Someone running rasps up and down the nerves and not missing a one.

More car horns blaring. Tires screeching. People screaming. Running away from me.

The world is so bright. Who turned up the sun?

Shouldn't it be warmer too then? Instead of cold like this?

Glass crashes.

Minds everywhere, but one stands out. A woman.

Whole being focused on me. Focused like I meditate focused. So intent on me it's like there isn't a person there at all. Just a single fixed thought.

I am this woman's hoop, and her bullet is her basketball.

There's also some swearing. But that's a sideline. Doesn't touch the focus.

Next shot. There has to be a next shot.

The mind is five hundred yards away. Crouched on top of Long Pine Savings and Loan.

Needs one more shot.

Can't see me past a brown Buick Skylark.

Has to abandon the kill. Try again later.

Get me later.

No.

No. You won't.

Pain all through me. Lava pain. White nova heat burning through my shoulder like it's trying to get to my racing heart before it manages to pump all my blood out of the crater where my shoulder used to be.

And I give all of that pain to the assassin.

I don't even know how, exactly. Nothing like coherence in my thoughts.

Just here's the pain. There's the mind. Smush them together.

I can hear her scream from here.

I echo it. Because I still have all that pain. Every drop. Sharing it doesn't take it from me.

I'm not the only one echoing it. Others around me scream too. A symphony of suffering.

I try to find more for the assassin anyway. Even though it doesn't diminish mine. I try to reach for my fear, but I can't find it past my pain.

Just as well. I've lost her mind now anyway. I can't feel her at all.

In fact, I can't feel anyone. I mean, I can *feel* them there, but they aren't important. Their identities. Their thoughts. They don't matter. Any more than the screaming matters, so I stop that too.

The tears keep coming, but they don't matter either.

Huh.

Now even the pain doesn't seem to matter so much. It's fading like the end of a song. Still there and still intense, but distant.

Footsteps running toward me. Concerned faces leaning over me.

"Rick! Are you all right?"

Stupid question, Agent Johnson. I'm fine. The pain is going somewhere else.

Pain, pain, go away.

Come again some other day.

I'd give you a smile, Agent Johnson, but I'm just a little spacey right now.

No. Not spacey. Just a little sleepy.

Yeah, that's it.

Sleepy.

I'll just put my head down and...

15

———

My mouth is dry.

Not nervous before a big kiss dry. More like cracked sidewalk in the summer heat dry.

My tongue feels puffy.

Someone packed my skull with cotton. A layer between me and the world.

Where the...

Oh.

Of course.

I'm in a hospital.

You would think I'd recognize that smell before anything else. Like alcohol and bleach judged an antiseptic contest and the winner got to climb up my nose.

I feel like the smell should bother me, but it doesn't. It's just there.

My eyes are gummy. Takes me a few tries to blink them. That should bother me too, but it takes too much focus just to make them blink. To get them to focus on what's around me.

It's a hospital room all right. Small. Private. Done in white and — what would Mom call that green? — pistachio, I think.

Maybe pale lime.

Clock on the opposite wall says it's ... nine ... thirty. Darkness outside my window says that must be p.m.

Handwriting on a white board takes me a moment to decipher. Swoop and swirl. Round like a loop.

There's a name in the loop. My nurse. Deb. She last came by at ... nine-oh-five.

That was recently, right?

I shift a little under the sheets. Hey. I *am* under sheets. Stiff, rough sheets. And I'm in one of those hospital gowns.

Someone saw me naked.

I start laughing. Not a loud, hearty laugh, but a half-giggle half-chuckle like a kid who heard something naughty. Stretches my lips out and hey!

My mouth is dry.

I start to look around and see an I.V. coming out of my arm. This is just so weird I stare at it. There's a tiny little needle poking into the back of my hand. And there's some clear liquid in a tube.

And yet my mouth is dry. Why is that?

Someone coming. A mind at the door intercepts. I have guards. Agents Templeton and Beauregard. And the person they're talking to is...

Agent Johnson.

I start chuckling again. Johnson. My life was saved by Agent Penis.

I start to lean forward laughing as the door opens, but my movement doesn't feel right. Something pulls at my left shoulder.

My heavily bandaged left shoulder.

I'm in the hospital.

I stop laughing.

"Good to see you awake," says Agent Johnson. He sounds droll, but he's smiling. "You gave us all a pretty bad scare."

"My mom—"

"Your parents are finally down in the cafeteria, eating. So's your friend Tony. They've all been here with you since you were admitted. Soon as we're done here I'll let them know you're awake."

"Done here?"

"Just a little debriefing." He turns around a hard metal chair and sits on it backwards. "What the hell were you thinking, stopping at Boomer's?"

"It's just what I do on the way home from a hike."

"And you didn't think to mention that?"

There's an answer somewhere in my head, but I can't quite find it. I'm tempted to find it in Agent Johnson's head. But his mind is swirling about a bunch of things and I don't want to know what.

I feel like there's an answer here somewhere though, if I can just find it.

"That's all right," he says. "I understand. It's just part of your routine. You didn't even think. Did you?"

I shake my head.

"Wish you'd thought to mention it. Could have stopped Swenson before she fired a shot and saved some wear and tear on your shoulder."

He looks at it more closely.

"How does it feel?"

"It doesn't. Maybe a little stiff and restrained."

"Sounds right. You were in surgery for hours. And you probably aren't done yet. Your parents have at least one specialist flying in."

"Did you get her? The assassin?"

Agent Johnson drums his fingers on the back of the chair while he thinks. I have more than enough attention on my shoulder to not pick up what he's thinking.

But I do pick up his aftershave. It's ... sporty. Doesn't suit him.

Doesn't mix right with the room smells either. In fact—

"It's the strangest thing," says Agent Johnson. "She appeared to have a rope ready to drop to the ground where she had a motorcycle waiting and no doubt a solid escape route.

"Except Agent Templeton saw her there at the edge of the rooftop of that savings and loan. Swenson grabbed her head and screamed. Templeton said it was the worst scream she ever heard, and between you and me Templeton has seen some shit.

"Anyway, then Swenson just fell. Looked unconscious before she hit the ground."

Agent Johnson arches an eyebrow at me.

"Hell of a thing. Wouldn't you say?"

"At least no one blew away half her shoulder."

"True. Still. Any chance you're going to tell me what happened there?"

"Pang of conscience? Aneurism?"

"Off the record."

His eyes are trying to bore into me. He's thinking about reporters. I mean, he's thinking about a lot of things, but he's *really* thinking about reporters. Guys with hats that have a Press card in the brim, and flip-top notepads.

Guys that are nothing like him.

And I'm in the hospital because I've been shot. The police had to have been notified. That means Agent Johnson is now here officially.

I don't try to hide the realization dawning all over my face. Not that I could do a good job of hiding it right now anyway.

Agent "Johnson" smiles and winks at me.

"Sorry," I say. "Sounds like a medical fluke to me, but I'm not a doctor."

"That's what I think too," he says with a sigh. "But it's my job to ask in a situation like this, because one time in ten thousand it might not be. Just like that weird synchronized scream from a crowd of panicked people. Must have been some kind of herd instinct."

Agent Johnson stands up.

"So, yes, we got Swenson. And since the money man appears to be dead, you should be free and clear once you get out of here."

He smiles at me.

"You might not make that date Friday night, though. Not if you need more surgery."

Unfortunately, whatever amazing painkillers they have me on don't help with that kind of pain. I hear Agent Johnson chuckle as I groan and press deeper into my pillow.

"Good luck to you, Rick. I left my card on your desk at home, in case you ever need me for anything." His face gets serious for a moment. "But I think we both hope you never do."

Then he smiles again. "Unless you want to help your country. Believe me when I say your Uncle Sam needs people like you."

That's what he leaves me with. And as I say goodbye I don't have the heart to tell him that I sincerely hope Uncle Sam doesn't have anyone like me working for him.

The thought of that red house in Alexandria frightens me more than just a little.

Agent Johnson was right.

I didn't make that date. But Isla Perkins was gracious about it on the phone. And she's willing to reschedule. In fact, if I were to judge by her tone, I'd say that getting shot and watched over by federal agents has made me even more of a curiosity to her.

Maybe it even helps my sex appeal. Can't tell. She was flirty on the phone, but that might be reflex.

It's been more than a week now since that chat with Agent Johnson, and I'm still in the freaking hospital. Mom and Dad and Tony are here every day, keeping me company until I'm ready to go home.

Physically, I mean. Mentally and emotionally I've been ready to go home for days. At least, I think I am. I mean, I know I'm going stir crazy in this little white and pistachio room that smells like the offspring of two different sterilizing products.

But emotionally, part of me just wants to curl up here and hide.

Mom and Dad want me to see a therapist for a while. Just to make sure I don't suffer any long term effects from someone trying to kill me. Not to mention killing more than half my friends.

It's probably a good idea. If I can figure out a way to discuss my situation without telling my headshrinker that I'm a mind-reader.

Bad enough that Agent Johnson knows. Or thinks he does. If he were certain, if he wanted to act or do any kind of follow-up, I'd have had to go into his mind and change it for him.

I am not going to spend every day in a little red house reading minds for Uncle Sam.

Fortunately Agent Johnson is willing to let his suspicions go, with the knowledge that if the weird shit every really hits the fan, I'm more likely to help him out if he doesn't rat me out now.

Sees it as a kind of long-term insurance that he never wants to cash in.

Speaking of the government, it's been days now, and the cops have yet to show up and ask me any questions. That kind of surprises me, but maybe it shouldn't. I guess Agent Johnson or my parents must have taken care of that angle.

Meanwhile, my left shoulder is an absolute mess. I'm missing more than a cubic inch of flesh, and the bullet tore up muscles, ligaments and bones. I have a second surgery coming up in a few days — if my healing continues on schedule — and after that I should finally, *finally* get to go home.

Oh, and I have one more surgery scheduled as a follow up in August, after which I'll practically go from the hospital to … wherever I'm living for my sophomore year. I don't know if Jamal set things up for the apartment transfer before…

Anyway, I wish I could have that third surgery sooner, but I guess I have to recover from the first two before I can handle the third.

I hope it does me some good. Gets me ready for some real physical therapy. Right now they say I may never get back full use of my arm.

Still, it could have been worse.

If Agent Johnson hadn't hit his car horn that first blast, I wouldn't have started to turn when I did. The bullet would have hit its mark. Right through the heart, like the others.

I'd be dead.

I'd shiver if it weren't for the pain meds.

Instead it took out my shoulder and spun me to the ground. Which made the head shot go just wide of its mark and hit the concrete wall of the building behind me.

Then I was on the ground and behind the cover of cars both parked and moving. Some of which held NSA agents.

Lots of panic from the bystanders, which may have helped. None of them were hurt. Or I guess I should say that none of them were shot. I think I may have done some psychic damage in there when I shared that scream. Maybe some spill-over when I sent out my pain.

Probably keeping the therapists of this town in business for years. Not to mention adding more than a little guilt to my plate.

Which isn't entirely fair. It's not like I was fully in control of myself at the time.

Yeah, that therapist Mom and Dad want to send me to is sounding better and better. I'll have to remember to tell Candi I'm seeing one of her future peers.

Nah. She must want to do research if Hollywood doesn't make a star out of her. Not very many neuropsychologists in clinical practice. As far as I know, anyway.

Jenna's been in touch by text. Checking up on me. Not as often as when I got out of the hospital after that coma last year, but she's pretty busy. She's got a research assistant gig studying the rocks of southeastern Montana.

Had to tell her it was a drive-by aiming for someone else, but that's just as well. No need to worry her.

Anyway, she's into another one of the assistants at the site. Steve. University of Montana guy. Shares her love of all things Geology.

Cool. Hope they're happy.

Me. Right now lying here in bed and convalescing sounds like the best thing in this or any other world.

Right now, I can't imagine anything important enough to need my attention.

Rick, do you have a moment?

Now is when Hyun-Ki Noh wants to talk? Now?

But of course.

I REACH OUT TO SAY HELLO TO HYUN-KI NOH AND FIND MYSELF IN A boardroom that smells like saffron. Twelve aggressive executive chairs around a big slate gray table in a room full of windows.

One window wall looks out over the skyline of New York. Another looks out over what looks to me like Tokyo. A Christ statue in the distance tells me the third is Rio de Janeiro. The fourth, I think, is Dubai.

Hyun-Ki Noh sits at one end of the table. His personal image profile is slim. Fit. And wearing an extremely expensive suit.

The ten side chairs are empty. I plop into a seat at the other end of the table. I'm amused to see that I'm wearing my traditional summer uniform of plaid shorts and a Three Coyotes tee shirt.

"So this is a formal chat?" I say.

"I didn't want to convey unearned familiarity." He places his hands on the table, palms down. "Just what exactly were you trying to draw me into?"

"I beg your pardon?"

"I can't help but notice that when your little group is not dying by bullets fired from high-powered rifles, you appear to be keeping company with federal agents."

"Yes," I say with a sigh, "well, it has been an unusual summer."

"Unusual?"

"WHAT DO YOU WANT ME TO SAY?" I'm on my feet now and ready to leave. "I just had to watch most of my friends get gunned down over one man's jealousy and megalomania. I'm alive and in the hospital *right now* only because one of those federal agents saved my life.

"Oh, yeah, and I helped capture an international assassin. Let's not forget that."

Hyun-Ki Noh is leaning back in his chair now, his eyes wide. I'm probably leaking all kinds of subtext all over him but I don't care.

And I'm not done.

"And did I once say, 'Hyun-Ki, I need your help?' or anything else that could possibly get construed as *drawing you in* to the havoc that my last couple of weeks have been?"

I drop back into that chair.

"I met a new telepath at a baseball game and tried to introduce you to my friends. I thought maybe we could expand our telepathic social circle, because I can tell you from personal experience it sucks to have no one to talk to about this stuff.

"It just happened that we met on the wrong fucking day. And if that means that you're going to sit there and judge me, or suspect me of some kind of weird political game, or just make me go through any more shit than I've already gone through, then you can go to hell and I'll go back to trying to heal.

"I just can't take one more telepath who thinks that having this knack means that everything in the world must revolve around them."

I'm pretty much out of steam at that point. I start rubbing my eyes with the heels of my palms, before it occurs to me that I can't even do that back in my body right now.

"The first telepath I ever met," says Hyun-Ki, "was my uncle. He taught me how to handle my power. How to adjust and how to fit in. And he also taught me to trade in secrets."

His nostrils flare in a sigh.

"My uncle was a bad, bad man. Another time I will send you memories of what he did to me. What he put me through.

"I needed years to get free of him. Sometimes I feel as though I'm still under his thumb. He had worked small controls in my brain while he taught me. I think they are all gone now, but..."

He shakes his head.

"I apologize for accusing you. It looked as though you were trying to involve me in some personal war. To use me, as my uncle did. I see now that I was wrong."

"I understand. I've seen just about every shade of gray from other telepaths, but morality seems to be harder for us than it is for other people."

"Not harder." He smiles. "It is a test of character. That is all. And you and I must be careful as we meet others."

"I don't just want to meet others."

Even in someone else's head I sound so tired I could just collapse unconscious. But I have to go on.

"I want to form a community. National. International. Worldwide, if we can do it. I want to bring all the telepaths of the world together. Unite us, so that we can help one another, as well as stem the tide of potential abuse.

"I don't want any telepath to awaken to their powers alone and afraid, the way I did. And I don't want innocents to suffer under the predations of people like your uncle, and like Stephen."

"That will require a lot of trust between us."

"I agree," I say with a nod. "We have a whole lot to talk about before we can get there. You and I both have to know for certain that we can trust each other."

I sigh and lean my elbows on the table.

"But before we can even get that far, I need to know if this sounds good to you."

Hyun-Ki Noh smiles.

"It does indeed."

EPILOGUE

TWENTY YEARS LATER

Doctor Rick Blackhall sits comfortably in his favorite armchair. Big enough to sink into and made from soft brown leather, the chair usually sits facing his antique teak desk, the showpiece of his personal study.

The room smells of old wood and books, which makes him happy. It is a holdout against the encroachment of technology, which the majority of the human race uses to do artificially what Rick can do telepathically.

Normally this is the place he goes to be alone with his own thoughts. But not today. Saturday mornings are for the new recruits.

There are twelve in the room with him now, spread across three matching couches around a large center table. Boys and girls, all from a spread of nations and backgrounds, all flown here for a small amount of private instruction with one of the founders of the World Telepathic Outreach.

And Rick has just given them a lot to process.

In a single burst of telepathy, he has shared with the twelve recruits the three most important experiences of his young life. The summer he developed telepathy. The trials and tribulations he suffered in college as he tried to form what became the short-lived Berkeley Telepathic Outreach.

And finally the dangers of those who would be jealous of their powers. The story of the assassin that almost killed him and did cripple his arm.

Oh, he regained much of its basic functionality. He was fortunate enough in that way. But he never built any real strength in his left arm again, and its mobility is ... limited.

Three bursts of memory. A moment to send, but though they all gain the basic information instantly, they will need hours or days to process the depths of what Rick learned in those early experiences. To take from his life the lessons that apply most to their own young lives.

"I know you will have many questions later," he says with a smile, "but what questions do you have now?"

"So," says a young Congolese teen, with short hair and wide eyes, "was that the start of the WTO? That first deep chat between you and Dr. Noh?"

"Not that day." Rick shakes his head slowly. "We needed time to come to know and trust one another. But that was the first seed that later blossomed."

"What happened with Jenna? And Isla?"

This question from a skinny little French girl on the cusp of puberty gets a laugh out of Rick.

"Someone always asks that. Jenna and I dated for a time after college, but our interests were too divergent. And I only knew Isla briefly.

"It was years before I met the woman I would later marry." Rick raises an eyebrow. "I'm afraid the story of how I met her is not germane to your telepathic development."

Titters through the room. *Was I ever that young?* he wonders.

"What about Terrence?" asks a pale boy with a Southern twang, with a somber aspect that says this question is very important to him.

"Terrence founded his own little group in Europe that focused entirely on secrecy. Sixteen telepaths spread across twelve countries.

They finally made contact with us seven years ago, and officially joined the WTO four years ago." Rick smiles. "Terrence and I had a lot of catching up to do."

"Why do we have to hide?"

A Japanese boy asks this one. Or perhaps Rick should think of him as a Japanese man. His face and body have filled in enough that he may have reached the age of majority. And the short cut of his black hair — shorter on the right than the left — is in fashion among the Japanese college students.

"The average person only thinks that two people should have power. Either that person alone, or someone that person has deemed 'trustworthy.'

"Telepathy doesn't work that way. We may have several working theories, but the truth is that we don't know how or why some people develop telepathy and others do not.

"Which means that those who *don't* would have to accept that there are simply those who *do*. There's no election. There's no recall process available to the non-telepathic. They get no say.

"That makes people nervous. Believe me. I've made a study of it."

Rick gestures to the place on his desk where his guests can see the set of six books he has published on the subject of power and group dynamics.

"With all too few exceptions, those who do not have telepathy will want to either control us, or kill us. Not for anything that we have done, but because they worry about what we might do."

"But we have our own rules. Our own code. We police each other."

The young Japanese man sounds certain that this is sufficient.

Rick shakes his head.

"Rules they did not choose. A code we could break without their knowledge. And as the question formed in ancient Rome, 'Who watches the watchmen?'

"No. We will continue to study. We will continue to make small cultural inroads. But for now and for the foreseeable future, we must remain a secret."

Other questions follow. None Rick has not learned to expect by now. The real questions will come next week or the week after. When they have all had the chance to truly understand what Rick shared with them.

But for now, as they file out — talking and sharing like one people instead of dividing along national lines — Rick can look upon yet another growing generation of telepaths and smile.

Perhaps the world is not ready for us yet, he thinks, *but we are ready for each other.*

And for now, that's enough.

THE BLACKHALL-GOTTSCHALK RULES OF TELEPATHIC CONDUCT

THE BLACKHALL-GOTTSCHALK RULES OF TELEPATHIC CONDUCT

General Rule 1: Telepathy is communication like speech. Anything that would be wrong to do verbally is probably wrong to do telepathically. Note that, in a telepathic sense, most people babble nonstop without knowing it. Shorthand: telepathy is thought speech.

General Rule 2: Owing to the risk of fear and exposure, a telepath should conceal his ability from others, and extend the same consideration to any other telepaths he might meet, should they exist. Shorthand: keep it quiet.

General Rule 3: The pressing needs of family and friends outweigh all other considerations. Shorthand: friends and family first.

Section 1: Casual Reading

1.1 Picking up the internal monologues and strong emotions of nearby people may be unavoidable, and doing so shall not be construed as the fault of the telepath. Information gained this way is to be treated as rumor or hearsay: unworthy of repeating in most cases, and unattributable in all other cases. Shorthand: it's not a crime to overhear.

1.2 Nothing learned by the method of 1.1 is to be considered verifiable truth. Surface thoughts can be deceptive. Shorthand: don't trust the monologue.

1.3 If, in the judgment of the telepath, a piece of information gained through the method of 1.1 suggests that a person intends to commit a crime, an act of terror, or harm to another person, that telepath shall be justified in using the method of 2.1 to investigate, followed by such other actions as may be appropriate. Shorthand: it's okay to be a hero.

1.4 If, through the method of 1.1, a telepath detects sexual interest in the telepath or in a close, personal friend of the telepath, from a desirable member of the appropriate sex, the telepath may, in his own judgment, use the method of 2.1 to investigate the candidate for suitability and compatibility. If the candidate is deemed suitable, the method of 2.1 may be employed to impress said candidate, or to otherwise gain information that would facilitate a hook up. Shorthand: love is not a crime.

1.5 Information gained through the method of 1.1 is acceptable to employ in sports, business, and all games of skill and chance. The telepath shall not be punished for possessing a natural advantage. However, let the telepath beware 1.2. Shorthand: play the people, not the cards.

Section 2: Deep Reading

2.1 Digging deep into a person's mind should only be done for a specific purpose, with due consideration given to the person's privacy. Information gained this way should not be shared, except as appropriate in the cases of 1.3 and 1.4. Shorthand: dig only for a reason.

2.2 Acceptable reasons to employ the method of 2.1 shall not include boredom, curiosity, or other entertainment. Shorthand: people are not books.

2.3 In addition to 1.3 and 1.4, acceptable reasons to employ the method of 2.1 include but are not limited to: training, business needs, pressing personal needs, and threats to health or safety. Shorthand: dig when it's urgent.

2.4 The reasons listed in 2.3 shall not be construed as to give the telepath carte blanche to go through a person's mind. The telepath shall confine his probing to subject matter relevant to the reason for the probe. Shorthand: stay on point.

2.5 Information gained from a person through the method of 2.1 can and will affect a telepath's interactions with that person. This shall not be regarded as a fault in the telepath. Shorthand: you're only human.

Section 3: Sending Thoughts

3.1 A telepath shall exercise caution when communicating directly with another person's mind. The thought recipient should be prepared, and not engaged in any dangerous or potentially dangerous activity at the time. The information should be sent in a clear, concise manner to avoid skewing reception. The telepath should also refrain from sending an excess of information in a single burst, for fear of overwhelming the recipient. Shorthand: say it safely.

3.2 All uses of the methods of 3.1 should be confined to those who already know about the telepath's ability. Violating this rule jeopardizes General Rule 2. Shorthand: keep it close.

3.3 It may be possible to employ the methods of 3.1 without alerting the recipient that a telepathic action has taken place. If so, the telepath must take care not to violate General Rule 2 or to accidentally veer into an application of the methods of 4.1. Shorthand: think carefully.

3.4 All thoughts, opinions, memories, and experiences of a telepath are to be regarded as the personal property of that telepath, even when they involve others. As such, a telepath is free to share those thoughts, opinions, memories, and experiences at his own discretion. Shorthand: you own yourself.

Section 4: Controlling Others

4.1 Whether subtly inserting an influential thought into a person's internal monologue or reaching deeper into the person's mind for direct control, this is the most powerful and dangerous ability of a telepath, and should be employed only with extreme caution. Shorthand: watch out for repercussions.

4.2 Acceptable reasons to employ the methods of 4.1 shall not include boredom, curiosity, entertainment (specifically including hook-ups), or petty justice or revenge. Shorthand: people are not toys.

4.3 Acceptable reasons to employ the methods of 4.1 shall include the following: training, pressing personal needs, threats to health or safety, and prevention of crimes or terrorist activities such as those learned about through 1.3. Shorthand: safety first.

4.4 There may exist valid reasons to employ the methods of 4.1 that are not listed in 4.3. If a telepath should encounter a situation that may qualify, he is to use the examples in 4.3 for comparison. If the situation qualifies, use of the methods of 4.1 may be employed and 4.3 expanded to include that situation. Shorthand: think before you take the wheel.

◊◊◊◊◊

For Melissa, the girl I didn't meet until years after college

ACKNOWLEDGMENTS

Many thanks to my amazing beta readers: Bill, Lori, Rob, Wendy

SIGN UP FOR STEFON'S NEWSLETTER

Stefon loves to keep in touch with his readers, and loves to keep you reading. The best way for him to do both is for you to sign up for his newsletter.

Sign up at http://www.stefonmears.com/join

If you sign up for Stefon's newsletter, you get...

- Monthly updates about his publishing and travel schedules
- His latest news, in brief, and answers to reader questions
- A free short story for signing up
- List-only offers and occasional specials
- Plus a free short story every month!

ABOUT THE AUTHOR

Stefon Mears doesn't want to end up in a certain Virginia house either. Stefon has more than thirty books to his credit, and he never stops writing. He earned his M.F.A. in Creative Writing from N.I.L.A., and his B.A. in Religious Studies (double emphasis in Ritual and Mythology) from U.C. Berkeley. He's a lifelong gamer and fantasy fan. Stefon lives in Portland, Oregon, with his wife and three cats.

Look for Stefon online:
www.stefonmears.com
himself@stefonmears.com